Captivating from the first page, Kim Clarke has written a story that brings awe and wonder to the normalcy of life. By seamlessly interweaving the wisdom of scripture, the narrative encourages readers to renew their devotion to prayer and hope in God. Clarke's writing is rich with imagery and historical details that delight and invite the reader into the adventure, leaving us to pray for our own waving receipts in the snow!

—Rev. Nahri Hong
Associate Pastor, GoodTree Church
Calgary, Alberta

Prayers and Paper Trails is a fun and engaging read. Kim Clarke deftly spins two story threads, intertwining them into a unique and intriguing plotline. Although the two female characters are literally and figuratively worlds apart, they both slowly mature in their understanding and practice of prayer and come to experience God on a deeper level.

—Dr. Susan Booth
Professor of Evangelism and Missions,
Canadian Baptist Theological Seminary and College
Cochrane, Alberta

PRAYERS & PAPER TRAILS

PRAYERS & PAPER TRAILS

KIM LOUISE CLARKE

Softcover ISBN: 978-1-4866-2777-6
Hardcover ISBN: 978-1-4866-2779-0
eBook ISBN: 978-1-4866-2778-3

Word Alive Press
119 De Baets Street Winnipeg, MB R2J 3R9
www.wordalivepress.ca

WORD ALIVE
—P R E S S—

Cataloguing in Publication information can be obtained from Library and Archives Canada.

To
Hannah and Philip
with love.
You make the world a brighter place.

ACKNOWLEDGEMENTS

THANK YOU, IAN, for your encouragement that propels me toward writing better. Your reading of my first drafts and valuable advice is always appreciated. Thank you for your understanding when I need to stare out of a window to process the actions of my fictitious characters. Thank you for your love and steadfastness throughout our many years.

Thank you, Philip, for sharing with me your expert help in all things writing. I value your creativity and opinions. And I love your determination and unwavering positiveness that I find so contagious. I treasure the chats we have about movies, character, plot, story, and on and on and on.

Thank you, Hannah, for your wonderful, fearless enthusiasm for life that inspires me. Thank you for listening to me when I talk about my story—yet again. I love our times laughing together as you help answer my off-the-wall questions. And your medical advice is very much appreciated.

Thank you, Marquita, for your faithful prayers and for being such a fan of all my writing. You are always there for me, to give me encouragement, moral support, and one more cup of coffee.

Thank you, Darcy and Gerson, for your genuine interest in my work, and for helping me understand more about weaponry and police procedures.

GoodTree Church is my church family, and I am blessed to be part of this vibrant fellowship where I am continually encouraged to grow in my relationship with Christ. I am grateful to be part of a fantastic group of Christian writers in the Calgary area, where honesty, trust, and laughter are part of every meeting. Thank you for your friendship and invaluable critiques! I also treasure being a member of InScribe Christian Writers' Fellowship, a rich fellowship of dedicated writers across Canada.

I greatly appreciate everyone at Word Alive Press for their advice, encouragement, and expertise in the publication process.

Thank you to each one of my readers. I hope you find this story to be entertaining, informative, and inspirational. My prayer is that you will grow in understanding God's love for you and His desire to answer your prayers.

As much as I strive to be accurate, I will make mistakes, and so any errors in this book are mine.

WIND

He... brings out the wind from his storehouses.
—Psalm 135:7

ONE

Calgary

JEAN-PAUL STOOD at the restaurant's entryway in his pants, shirt, and jacket—each piece a perfect blend of wool, linen, and silk. One might describe him as dressed to kill, but instead he had dressed to dine in a fine French restaurant; the killing had been done earlier that afternoon, in his haute couture jeans and quality cotton T-shirt. He'd had a busy day; having not eaten since breakfast at the hotel, he was looking forward to a substantial meal.

The young hostess at La Vie en Ville greeted him with a shy smile.

"*Bonsoir, monsieur.*"

Jean-Paul gave a slight nod in acknowledgement.

In addition to being a handsome middle-aged man, Jean-Paul appeared wealthy, like most of the restaurant's clientele. The hostess glanced up at his brown eyes and manicured goatee, taking a few seconds longer than she probably meant to. She asked him about a reservation, but none had been made.

"*Ça va bien,*" she remarked. "We have lots of room this evening."

She led Jean-Paul to a small, linen-covered table with a clear view of the darkening street. Once seated, he took in the last evidence of the September sunset. The view, partially blocked by downtown high-rises, gave him only glimpses of orange. But it was the wind, lifting leaves into a frenzy, that stole his attention. Mesmerizing movements. Branches losing more and more leaves in the vigorous gusts.

His wine arrived and the sauvignon rouge went down easily as he sipped and thought about the day. Almost everything about his assignment had gone as expected. A clean shot to the heart. The target, a businessman in a parkade, had meant nothing more to him than his seventy-thousand-euro fee, plus an additional five for travel expenses. A rather low fee for a low-risk job.

Jean-Paul swirled his red wine and watched it spin around the crystal. His mind remained in the parkade, processing the sequence of events.

Another assignment completed. And yet, not all had gone perfectly. The target, peering down at his car keys, had suddenly shot his head up toward the pillar Jean-Paul hid behind. He'd even paused, staring straight ahead as if waiting for the bullet. An easy and perfect shot.

But what had made him look?

Jean-Paul was convinced he'd made no sound, despite the close range. Using a silencer, he'd come to believe that silent accuracy was his expertise. Jean-Paul thought himself to be one of the best snipers in the world.

A doubt lingered, though. Had he somehow slipped? Made a slight noise?

He finished his first glass of sauvignon too quickly, as if swallowing these thoughts of losing his edge, getting a bit careless, growing old.

He poured another glass from the half-litre on the table and took a mental survey of his two-year career to shore up his sense of pride and accomplishment. How many assignments had he completed now? He silently listed eleven cities he had visited rather than count the number of people he'd killed.

When he'd first agreed to take on a few assignments, he had been told that the targets were known to be the worst in the criminal world. They deserved what they got. But Jean-Paul wasn't naïve. Maybe some deserved a bullet. Maybe others didn't. He thought it best to remain indifferent and obtain only the necessary information to accomplish the job.

Nearing the age of forty-six, he envisioned working as a hit-man for at least a decade to reap the financial benefits. The money he amassed was more than he had ever imagined he'd make.

He touched the edge of his collar, appreciating the soft fabric, and the fact that, without hesitation, he could buy a shirt for five hundred euros, and a double-breasted wool jacket for three times that much.

But his job provided more than financial freedom; it gave him a position where he could excel. Yes, he was excellent, and people respected excellence. Being his own boss was also a huge benefit.

The arrival of his appetizer interrupted his thoughts and he delved into the *vichyssoise*. Not bad, but he certainly had tasted better in Paris. The beef bourguignon followed, with its steaming aroma. He gave it the same verdict—not bad, not great. When it came to beef bourguignon, no one, not even a Parisian chef, could compare with his mother.

Halfway through his entrée, he paused to consider the city in which he found himself. He had been to Canada before—Toronto and Montreal—but here, "out west" as they said in Calgary, a kind of quiet had descended over the city's core. A city of just over a million and yet calm. Too calm.

He glanced out the window where the streetlights and head-lights of passing cars revealed more leaves being whipped up by the wind. Although warm and comfortable, he shivered and looked forward to returning to Paris in the morning.

After he finished his meal, he motioned to the waiter for the bill. "*Oui, monsieur. Un moment.*"

Upon receiving the bill, Jean-Paul handed the waiter seven twenty-dollar bills. The waiter made a quick calculation, under-standing that no change would be necessary, and smiled at the thirty-percent tip.

Jean-Paul rose and headed toward the door, stopping briefly to button up his jacket. The waiter hurried over with his receipt. Jean-Paul didn't want the receipt but took it anyway, to avoid any fussy interaction.

As he opened the door to exit, he heard the hostess say, "*Au revoir, monsieur.* Don't get blown away!"

He grimaced. Having been in Calgary two days, he realized that the people here lived as though the weather demanded some consideration every moment. He glanced back at her, having changed his grimace to a smile, and said, "*Merci. Au revoir.*"

When he left the sheltered restaurant doorway, receipt in hand, the wind collided with him rather than giving him any kind of embrace. The surprise chill bit into his bones, despite the quality of his wool jacket.

Then, as if on a mission, the wind whipped the receipt from Jean-Paul's hand. The paper twirled above his head, out of reach, not that he made any attempt to retrieve it.

He lifted his coat collar to fold around his neck and stuffed his hands into his pockets. Forceful gusts followed him, blowing his dark hair with its bits of grey into a chaotic mess. With his head bent, braced against the wind's attack, he made his way along several blocks to the five-star hotel.

"A bit windy out there tonight, sir," said the young hotel usher, holding open the heavy lobby door.

Jean-Paul wondered whether the man had asked a question or made a statement. Either way, trying to hide his irritation, he returned a slight nod and faint smile. He reminded himself of the importance of appearing pleasant, and most of all—forgettable.

Finally out of the wind, he strolled through the calm, spacious lobby. He slowed his steps to take in the plush carpets, marble pillars, and rich colours. It almost convinced him he was back in Paris. Although many Parisian structures boasted a long and rich history, Jean-Paul appreciated that this one at least made the most of its mere one-century existence.

He took the elevator to his fourth-floor room. After drawing the drapes to block out the night, he settled in for the evening. Comfortable in the corner armchair, he thumbed through his magazine on modern French architecture while enjoying a rich amber-coloured port.

Just because Jean-Paul had left an eighteen-year career in architecture didn't mean it no longer held any interest for him. He would always appreciate the field's creativity. He held good memories of his time designing, sketching, and finding creative solutions to deal with space and planning issues. But the time to do those things he loved had dwindled as other aspects of the work took over: unreasonable supervisors, endless meetings, difficult clients, arguments over budgets and timelines... his career had morphed into a litany of monotony and emptiness, hassle and frustration.

After a few minutes reading about a new apartment development in Paris's fourteenth arrondissement, Jean-Paul stopped to pour more port. He felt relaxed. When he had booked his flights the week prior, he'd searched for a return flight this very evening, but the local airport had offered him nothing. He admitted that he wasn't in any kind of terrible situation; he could enjoy an evening of relaxation in a quiet city before the long return flight in the morning.

He scanned the pleasant room and once again, as though needing assurance, dwelt on his transition from architecture to his current role of assisting people in dealing with their *rightful* revenge. He had achieved such status in this branch of organized crime that he could turn down any job. He was the one whisking himself away to the next assignment, the next city, the next country. No one controlled him. He called the shots—literally.

As Jean-Paul returned to his magazine, the wind howling outside the window, he couldn't help smiling at his play on words.

· · ·

The next morning, a sunny Friday, Jean-Paul left the hotel early. Before stepping into his taxi, he looked up into the solid block of blue sky above the city and felt the pleasant breeze. He took in this final scan of the city's intriguing skyscrapers, then continued on his way.

By mid-morning, he was seated comfortably in business class as the 747 rose over the chaos surrounding a downtown parkade cordoned off with yellow police tape, over the morgue where a prominent businessman now lay dead, and over a little piece of paper that had been blown into a hedge overnight after skittering down Seventh Avenue the previous evening; it was crushed under the weight of a heavy boot and transported up onto the floor of a city bus.

TWO

Calgary

HAZEL HEARD THE chirpy chimes at six o'clock in the morning and reached for her phone to silence the alarm. She rose out of bed looking forward to another predictable day.

Each morning after getting dressed for work, she dedicated fifteen minutes, sometimes even twenty, to spend with God. Hazel read a short story with a spiritual application from a devotional, then looked up the applicable scripture references. To conclude her time with God, Hazel said a silent prayer, thanking God for the day and asking for strength, wisdom, and guidance. Other days, she varied the requests and asked for patience, grace, and endurance. It depended on what words came to mind.

Before leaving her apartment to head to the bus stop, she checked herself in the bathroom mirror, not wanting to leave with muffin crumbs or a touch of yogurt on her face. She reached for a brush and ran it through her shoulder-length chestnut hair. She liked it that colour, feeling it suitable for a fifty-five-year-old woman who wanted to hide the oncoming grey. And the length meant she could tie it back or clip it up into a stylish bun—not that she ever did.

As she walked to the bus stop, Hazel considered her approach to the workday. Which accounts should she delve into first?

Maybe I'll concentrate on outstanding invoices.

Regardless of what she decided, she anticipated a calm, semi-challenging, enjoyable day sitting at her desk.

During the thirty-five-minute bus ride downtown, she stared out the window, her thoughts still hovering over her imagined work.

Every time her bus reached a certain overpass, without fail, Hazel's eyes abandoned whatever she'd been staring at to gaze west toward the Rocky Mountains, always hoping their magnificence would be visible, but knowing that clouds or morning haziness often obscured them, as they did this morning.

Hazel exited the bus and walked along Sixth Avenue to her office on the main floor of the Bernard Building. The fact of it being September gave her a bounce in her step. September 30 would mark another fiscal year-end for the Evergreen Printing Company. Like an astronomer's excitement over the lining up of planets, Hazel thrilled at the lining up of assets and liabilities. She loved seeing columns and rows harmoniously displayed on a consolidated balance sheet. Soon she would reach another perfect twelve-month culmination of dedicated work.

She loved her job.

Hazel faltered a bit in her stylish low heels as she turned the corner onto Fourth Street and found herself greeted by yellow tape sectioning off the lower level of a parkade.

Oh right, she remembered. *So this is where it happened.*

Her routine of listening to the news at seven o'clock each morning had her well-informed. She already knew there had been a murder the previous night.

I wonder who he was. Shot in broad daylight. My goodness!

Most people walking past likely wondered about the violence that had occurred, but Hazel did more than wonder. Out of habit, she silently released a prayer to God. A prayer for the grieving man's family. For justice to be done. For the bad guy to be caught.

It's not that she prayed with indifference, for she wanted all those things to happen. But what could she do about an incident so serious and violent other than pray?

Doing so brought back the lightness in her step. Now it was up to God to do whatever he wanted. Hazel continued walking, giving no further thought to the situation. She had done her bit.

Upon entering the Bernard Building, she headed toward the glass doors of Evergreen Printing on the main floor. Minutes later, in the staff room, she prepared coffee, ready to begin another day in the office. She wasn't aware of who else had arrived for work. She didn't much care to know about the employees in the back, the ones who prepared and printed customers' orders. She had very little interaction with them and didn't concern herself with the printing project. All that mattered was that the other employees did their jobs so she could sit in her tidy office near the front and keep accounts balanced and the payroll rolling.

Midmorning, Hazel returned for a second cup of coffee. But instead of returning to her office, she walked down the hallway that led to the front reception area to check on her coworker Maddie.

She admired the space, having helped her boss, Anthony Lee, pick out the black-and-white landscapes that hung on the grey walls above the black faux leather sofa chairs. It had taken fifteen years to convince Mr. Lee to spend a little money bringing the office into the third decade of the twenty-first century. Even though many things had changed in the world, with so much being accomplished online, customers still dropped in from time to time and they needed to see some signs of the business's success.

Maddie sat at the stool behind the front counter, her back toward Hazel. The strands of pink mixed into the new receptionist's naturally light brown hair robbed the reception area of its tranquillity, Hazel thought. The woman's lime-green sweater also didn't help.

Hazel stood and watched Maddie at work for a few seconds, tentatively typing on her computer and scanning sheets of paper. On days when business dragged, Hazel often handed

Maddie accounting tasks to keep her busy. Hazel appreciated the strengths Maddie had exhibited so far in the six weeks she'd been working at Evergreen. Whether by phone, email, or talking to customers in person, she had a pleasant demeanour. Hazel admired how she could easily chat people up about anything and everything.

Accounting, however, was not her forte. She didn't have a clue what she was doing.

"So, Maddie, how's it going?"

Maddie jumped and her arm, adorned with bracelets, shot up to steady herself before she could answer. Hazel marvelled at her own ability to startle others, though she never intended it. She was just a quiet person.

"Oh, man, you really scared me! Umm… it's going okay," Maddie said; the inflection at the end of the sentence seemed to indicate otherwise. "I can't seem to find those invoices you were asking about. I was about to come and see you."

Hazel set her coffee down and took the time to point out various online spreadsheets and refer to this or that piece of paper. Being so near, she caught the scent of Maddie's fresh minty coconut body lotion. It brought to mind a confusing scene of snow-covered evergreens running alongside a stretch of beachside palm trees.

Once she felt Maddie could continue fine on her own, Hazel gazed at the floor-to-ceiling windows, reflecting on the fact that she didn't much appreciate their fishbowl effect. Poor Maddie must feel like she was on display every hour of the day.

When she returned to her own desk, confined cozily within her office's four grey walls, she tried to get back to work. But her thoughts lingered on Maddie. She liked the young woman. In her early twenties, Maddie had already accumulated three years of administrative experience before coming to Evergreen. She'd even managed to rent a basement suite with friends.

Not an easy thing to achieve in this inflated economy, she considered.

But she questioned how much Maddie liked her in return.

I probably come across to her as an old cow.

Hazel gathered the discipline to concentrate on her work, and the afternoon flew by once she began.

At 4:56 p.m., Hazel noticed Maddie pass her office door to retrieve her jacket from the staff room. On her way, Maddie made the mistake of looking into Hazel's office and making eye contact.

"So did you make any progress with those invoices?" Immediately Hazel regretted sounding like a nagging mother and wondered why she didn't just tell Maddie to have a nice weekend.

"Well, I kinda have some of them sorted out. I'll get back at it on Monday if things aren't busy at the front."

Hazel tried to lighten things up. "Okay, no problem. Have a good weekend. Oh, and be careful of parking lots. You heard about the man they found shot? A businessman killed yesterday just a few blocks away. Young. Just in his fifties."

"Well, no, I hadn't heard. But I'll be careful. Thanks, Hazel."

Murder, Hazel thought to herself, shaking her head. *What a great way to lighten things up. All the same, I hope she appreciates my concern.*

It used to bother Hazel that Maddie habitually left several minutes early—that is, until she had figured out the reason. Being a Friday, all the young receptionist wanted to do was leave the office before anything could hold her back. For example, before a fellow employee could ask her about an order. Or before a chatty customer could call.

The important thing for Maddie was to get beyond that glass door. The weekend was calling.

Understanding this, Hazel now allowed herself to dismiss those few Friday minutes when Maddie abandoned her post. The phone rarely rang at that time of day anyway. After all, by five o'clock most everyone had vanished.

Hazel closed out her accounting files, shut down the laptop, and tidied a desk that needed no tidying. She then picked up her Inspirational Quotes desk calendar, a Christmas gift from her friend Julie, and reread the quote for September 9: "I'm not getting older. I'm becoming a classic." She couldn't help but hear Julie's voice speaking the words. With a roll of her eyes and a smile, she tore off the piece of paper, turned it over, and clipped it to an accumulation of scrap note paper.

She left her office, stopping to ensure that the coffee machine had been switched off; she never trusted the other employees to remember. Miraculously, though, some faithful employee had turned it off this time and taken care of the stewed remains in the pot.

On her way out, Hazel stopped at Mr. Lee's doorway. He was only six years her senior, although he looked a lot older. His arthritis had slowed him down in recent years, although mentally he remained sharp.

He sat at his desk, seemingly in no hurry to leave his little empire. If anything, he was happy to stay late on a Friday evening, which made Hazel feel okay about her life, since she didn't have any reason to dash out the door either.

She wished him a wonderful weekend and turned to leave.

Before leaving, she stopped at the counter in the reception area to straighten a few things for Maddie. She positioned the stapler so it sat parallel to the notepads and disposed of a crumpled piece of paper on the floor. Then, with a heavy sigh, she opened the glass door to walk into yet another adventure-less weekend. The weekends never called for Hazel, not anymore.

THREE

Calgary

HAZEL WALKED BACK down the street the way she had come, past the parking lot, which was no longer cordoned off. The parkade entry looked as it should—unremarkable, as if nothing had happened.

Rush hour was getting underway and Hazel knew her bus would arrive soon. She often walked out of her way to catch the bus one stop earlier, to ensure she got a window seat. Today was no different. She settled in next to the window and began watching the people outside, some standing and waiting while others walked with great strides to get somewhere.

As the bus made its way along Fifth Avenue, Hazel stared blankly, focusing on nothing specific. She wasn't in a particularly good mood and tried to trace the source of the problem.

She kept coming back to Maddie, knowing that the young woman herself wasn't the issue. It was how Hazel felt around her. Simply put, Maddie made her feel old. An old fuddy-duddy. In all her fifteen years employed at Evergreen, she couldn't remember feeling like this about herself at work until recently.

I'm not old, she told herself. *Not really. Sure, I'm the oldest employee there, but that doesn't make me old. Ninety-nine is old, for Pete's sake.*

For years, Hazel had viewed herself as an asset. Someone who brought maturity and experience to the company. Someone who had needed expertise.

But when Hazel thought about the company itself, she realized that business was not what it had been a decade ago. It certainly hadn't been robust for a long time. The economic cycle of boom and bust seemed to have lost its rhythm, getting stuck on bust.

I shouldn't worry. I'm needed at Evergreen and Mr. Lee knows that. Besides, the economy will pick up—it always does, eventually. I'm sure I have many, many more years of working there.

After a few more stops, the bus filled until it was standing room only. Within hearing distance, two young businessmen stood with their arms lifted high to grasp the bus's handles. They swayed as the bus took its corners, but the movement never interrupted the flow of their conversation; they were talking about a new technology company soon to set up its headquarters in Calgary. Their voices held optimism.

The eavesdropping comforted Hazel. Yes, the economy was picking up. She'd be fine in her job. She would likely stay there until her retirement at sixty-five. Ten more years.

Having calculated her income for the next decade, plus pension and investment income, she believed she could retire quite reasonably. Certainly not in luxury, but she would be okay if she kept her spending conservative. She felt a touch of contentment over her handling of her personal finances.

Maybe I could settle myself in Paris or Barbados, she mused, allowing herself to daydream. *Or at least live somewhere exotic six months of the year.*

She smiled at such silliness, knowing she would never accumulate that much money. Besides, travelling came with all sorts of risks. What would she do if she needed extended medical care while out of the country? Or dental surgery? Cementing herself in Calgary, where she'd had the same family doctor for decades, and the same dentist for almost as long, even the same shoe repair shop, oozed security and safety. Besides, she had never been fond of travelling. She'd visited other parts of Western Canada and the northern United States but preferred her calm life in Calgary.

Daydreaming aside, the thought of retirement terrified her. She didn't believe money would be the problem. Rather, she was worried about having a purpose. If she were honest with herself, she would be lost without her job. What would she do all day, all week, all month? She already struggled to endure the weekends, spending too much time in her personal void. Friday nights weren't too bad, giving her a night to relax after a busy work week. But Saturdays? That's when Hazel felt lost. Unanchored. She busied herself with bits of housework, reading, shopping, and the occasional stroll. At least Sundays were somewhat better, with church filling the morning.

She felt a bit sorry for herself. Predictably, the weekend would drag, full of comfort and dread in partnership. The fleeting thought of finding a new crime series to stream gave her a little jolt of happiness.

The bus crossed the Bow River, made its way up Centre Street, then turned onto Fourth Street to arrive in Hazel's neighbourhood. The bus was now only a quarter full as it passed the familiar strip mall and duplexes. She gathered her purse and adjusted her jacket, getting ready to stand.

That's when she noticed a small piece of paper on the floor by her feet. Probably a receipt. Such a rare thing these days.

She bent down to pick it up.

Yup, a receipt.

How could someone lose this? she asked herself. *It's handed to you, then you put it in your purse or pocket. How difficult can that be, for Pete's sake? Careless. That's what people are. They don't care. They don't care about paper. They don't care about keeping track of things. No wonder people are in debt.*

The least she could do was to drop it into a garbage can or recycle bin. Along with her prayer that morning about the latest act of violence in her city, this would be another good deed for the day.

Her bus stop on Fourth Street was comprised simply of a pole with a metal sign, indicating the Number 2 bus. The stop had no enclosed shelter to protect transit riders from wind, rain, or snow. Neither did it have a bench, nor an attached metal trash bin so one could dispose of things like dirty receipts. Hazel had once called the city about this and been informed that a proper shelter was on the agenda. Not wanting to be a bother to anyone, she'd never called back. That was more than a year ago.

Having left the bus, Hazel stood still to glance over the receipt's details, still legible despite a partial boot print. Someone had ordered a meal at La Vie en Ville the night before.

Let's see… there's something unpronounceable, then bourguignon, and something else, maybe wine? Wow, what an expensive place.

Hazel stuffed the receipt in her pocket as the wind picked up. She walked parallel to the strip mall, making her way first to the pedestrian crosswalk and then a collection of apartment buildings across the street. She followed the curved sidewalk to her building's front door.

Inside she emptied her mailbox of its usual flyers. Most people considered it junk mail, but not Hazel. These paper advertisements had the potential to offer her interesting information. One never knew which might contain something of value. She enjoyed the different weights and textures of the paper. She liked the glossy print but felt the matte finish had a more calming effect.

Her ingrained delight of paper had begun when Hazel was just eight years old. The third-grade class had taken a field trip to a paper factory in the northeast part of the city. A bored employee had toured the twenty-five students past aisles of machinery, explaining how a pad of paper comes into existence. Hazel had been anything but bored. If anything, her face had beamed the entire time.

At tour's end, each student had received two small pads of paper, varying in length and width. These were the leftovers, dregs and scraps, and Hazel had treasured them. She'd considered that to be one of the most glorious days of her entire school career.

Hazel strolled toward the elevator, scanning the advertisements and discarding several pamphlets in the nearby recycle bin. It would have been a logical place to rid herself of the receipt, which now lay forgotten in her coat pocket.

Before she could press the button for the elevator, she was interrupted by her neighbour, Praveen, who approached with the jolliness of Santa Claus.

"Hello there, Hazel!"

She never knew when she would run into Praveen at the mailboxes. Over the seven years since he'd moved into the building, their paths often crossed. His bubbly demeanour never failed to make her feel warm and connected.

As usual, they chatted about the weather, getting old, and the price of food. And as usual, she felt a sense of camaraderie in their sharing the same adversities in life.

Since Praveen often travelled, Hazel asked for an update on where he had been lately. She felt envious of his adventurous spirit.

Today he shared about his plans to visit Montreal in late October.

"It's a great city for walking around," Praveen said. "And my youngest brother lives near Mount Royal. Such a beautiful area. He's already compiling a list of new restaurants he'd like to try out when I come. Have you ever been there, Hazel?"

"Can't say that I have. But it sounds exciting. Maybe one day."

After a few more minutes of chatting, she watched him head down the hallway to his apartment on the main floor. As he walked, she calculated his age. Praveen had once talked about his family giving him a grand celebration on his eightieth birthday. How many years ago had that been? Four years? Nope. Five.

Eighty-five years old, she decided. *He's getting up there, but he sure isn't letting his age stop him at all.*

Once in her apartment on the third floor, Hazel changed out of her taupe pants and black top into comfortable sweatpants and a T-shirt. She then opened the fridge door to consider her dinner options. When she placed a plate of leftover meatballs, rice, and carrots in the microwave, thoughts of beef bourguignon came to mind.

And she remembered the receipt.

While the food zapped and crackled, she retrieved the piece of paper from her jacket pocket and studied it more carefully, picturing herself indulging in such a lavish dinner. Something tastier, certainly, than what she was about to eat.

Boeuf bourguignon was obviously the main entrée, but what on earth was vichyssoise? Probably something high in calories, but wonderful. And Bordeaux—a wine, a port?

She gave herself a moment to imagine the richness of not just the food but the restaurant itself.

I wonder if entering that kind of place feels like stepping out of Calgary's grey concrete and entering the plush interiors of Paris. I wonder if Édith Piaf's voice can be heard singing softly in the background—

The beeping of the microwave brought Hazel out of her imaginings. The receipt found its way into her recycle bin under the sink.

Hazel sat on the couch with her quickly cooling supper to watch the local news. It provided no update on the identity of the businessman who'd been murdered, nor any hint of the murderer.

After immersing herself in the tragedies of real people, she left the screen to prepare a small plate of veggies and dip. She returned to the couch and entered the lives of fictional people—some committing crimes, others trying to solve them. Despite her muttering, the characters on the screen never heeded her advice. She had little sympathy for detectives who never waited for backup.

The weekend had now begun in earnest.

Her weekends hadn't always been a desert-wandering of binge-watching. Back in May, Hazel would have found herself occupied far more meaningfully. She and Julie would have been up to something fun. Something worthwhile. Something silly. Their friendship had begun in university and spanned three decades. It had survived Julie's tumultuous marriage of eighteen years and the death of both sets of their parents.

When Julie's daughter Heather had come down from Edmonton, she'd easily slipped into the fun events the two friends had planned. Their weekends had often involved going for lunch at new restaurants, shopping in trendy areas, watching good movies, and attending church activities.

One pastor had referred to them as the *dynamic duo*, but most everyone viewed Julie as the leader, the instigator, the encourager. She would be the one to say, "Why not?" And Hazel and the other women in church would hesitantly go along with it. Because of Julie, the Saturday morning women's Bible study had been going strong for years. A church hiking group had started up last year.

Then, three months ago, Psalm 116:15 had become the most perplexing scripture verse to Hazel: *"Precious in the sight of the Lord is the death of his faithful servants."*

But Hazel couldn't see anything precious about Julie's death.

Couldn't God have caused that SUV driver to hit a streetlight rather than Julie's car? she demanded. *Why couldn't Julie have been the one to emerge with only a few bruises?*

If she'd had the power, Hazel would have written out the scenario so much differently, but she couldn't. She couldn't change anything. She remained completely powerless in the unfolding of life's events.

She felt the least God could have done was allow the weather on the day of the funeral to be stormy, matching her newly chaotic life. But he hadn't. Instead the sun shone brilliantly, getting no competition from any clouds.

Over the summer, Hazel had struggled to find comfort from the words offered by her friends and pastors. Isaiah 55:8 seemed to be the foundation underlying everyone's encouragement: *"For my thoughts are not your thoughts, neither are your ways my ways."* But Hazel struggled to find solace in God's declaration.

* * *

Hazel's quiet Friday night was followed by an uneventful Saturday, bringing Hazel to Sunday morning. She drove to church and parked her car a block away, since every spot in the parking lot had been taken.

She found her usual place in the back pew. Once again she had managed to arrive in time to avoid what she had considered over the past few months to be nothing more than monotonous preservice chitchat.

With just a few moments to pass before the service began, Hazel waited. She longed for the good old days of the church bulletin, when she could hold a pamphlet in her hand, read of upcoming events, and occupy these few moments. Back then, she'd been able to exercise control over what she read, but technology had put a stop to that. With the announcements now projected onto the screens, she had no choice of what to read, and no control over how long she took to read it.

I wonder when churches first started printing bulletins, she mused. *And where? Europe, I'd imagine. Are there any churches left in the world that still print Sunday bulletins? Probably not.*

As the service began, Hazel did all the things expected of a faithful congregant. When the congregation stood to sing, she followed suit. She closed her eyes for the congregational prayer and did her best to listen to the sermon.

At the closing of the benediction, Hazel made a quick exit. She had no desire to remain in the foyer, which would no doubt soon be filled with chatter, especially since September had arrived. The foyer always swelled with excited talk of how people had busily occupied their summers. Families had returned from vacations. Kids had gone back to school. Sunday school and Bible studies had all resumed their normal schedules.

Since Julie's death, though, Hazel felt more and more like an observer rather than a participant in the church she had attended for two decades. When the service ended, all she looked forward to was returning home; there was never anything exciting there, but at least she was guaranteed solace.

On her way back to her car, she realized that the wind had picked up. Other than a cool breeze, Hazel didn't much like wind. It disturbed everything, blowing away one's tranquillity and calm, allowing disarray and disorganization to rule. And it never failed to render Hazel's hair a dishevelled mess. Most irritating!

But since she was only going home, it didn't matter what she looked like.

In the afternoon, Hazel curled up on her couch to read a crime thriller. One of the book's characters, a thief, had just unwittingly become a murderer. That hadn't been his plan, though, and he now tore down a back alley in confused panic—

Hazel's cellphone rang. She jumped, dropping the paperback and losing her place.

"Hazel, Aunt Peggy died last week," the voice on the other end of the line informed her. "David just called me. The funeral's this Wednesday. Will you be able to make it?"

"Oh! Hi Fran… yes, I suppose I can make it."

"Good. I'll text you the info. See you then."

Hazel wanted to add something, but Fran had already hung up. Given the chance, she would have said something like, "We haven't seen either David or Aunt Peggy for so long. I can't remember when the last time was. Do you recall? Do you know if she was sick? What did she die of? I wonder how old she was…"

But her conversations with Fran were rare—and when they did happen, they were brief. Just the facts. No chatting about Aunt Peggy, whom neither sister had really known. After the death of their parents twenty years before, she and Fran no longer kept in touch with their mom's only sister, Peggy, nor her son David. The weak family connection had grown even weaker over the years.

She felt annoyed at the prospect of having her upcoming workweek interrupted by a funeral, especially with the year-end reports she had to complete. And the fact that she would have to spend time with her sister made it extra painful.

Hazel could picture it now. After the funeral service, she would be standing with Fran and their cousin David—hopefully they'd recognize him somehow. While nibbling on little crustless sandwiches, she and David would be forced to listen to Fran's oh-so-important stories about what she had accomplished in life, and what they hadn't.

Sitting on the couch, three days from the funeral, Hazel already felt the frustration of being with her sister. That feeling always came with a jab of envy. She'd eye Fran's expensive outfit, undoubtedly bought at full price. Her big jewellery wouldn't only flash but also match her outfit, her shoes, and her purse. Everything was always very matchy-matchy; Fran controlled everything about herself. The conversation would revolve around her important life. And would Hazel be able to share anything about her own life? Of course not. Fran would dominate the stage.

Hazel had conceded years ago that she would never measure up to Fran. She would never attain her competence, sophistication, wealth, or contributions to church and community. The woman was already involved in every committee that had ever existed.

It's a miracle she still believes in God, someone more important and in control of all things… and it's not her. Imagine that! I wonder how she pictures life's hierarchy. She probably sees God first, barely, with herself as second-in-command. And the rest of the world? Way down at the bottom.

This painful road down memory lane called for a cup of coffee.

With a steaming, aromatic coffee in hand, Hazel approached her balcony's glass door and leaned her shoulder against it. She watched the leaves, dancing and swirling under the wind's control. Across the street, clumps of tall natural grasses served as Hazel's de facto weathervane. At the moment, they were forced to bow to the southeast.

The curtain fell back into place and Hazel decided to make herself a sandwich for dinner. She would end the weekend watching the evening news and anticipating Monday, when she could once again step into her world of logic, balance, and routine.

But she couldn't help but anticipate Thursday. By then all this business with the funeral would be over with and she could continue with her work.

Hazel had always liked her accounting job but had never hidden herself in it before, at least not until Julie's death. Over the summer it had grown to become a refuge. A reliable place, just as reliable as the inescapable calculation that twelve times twelve always equals 144. Her work world was now her cocoon—warm, predictable, and organized… but oh so small.

FOUR

Paris

A FEW DAYS had passed since Jean-Paul's return to Paris. Back to his prestigious Haussmann-style apartment in the seventh arrondissement.

In his chic surroundings, where ceilings rose high and natural light flooded in, he sat on his white leather sofa. He could have looked outside at the colourful fall leaves or at the distant golden glow of the dome of Les Invalides. But his eyes remained on the pattern of the Persian carpet, thinking he should call his mother. Of all the people in his life, Brielle remained the only person he cared about. All others flitted across his life, leaving no reason to maintain connection. They were insignificant—except for Brielle, who didn't pry into his life. At least not too much.

He picked up his phone.

"*Bonjour, Maman.* Yes, back in town for a while now. Not sure when the next meeting will be, but I'd love to take you out for dinner sometime this week. What evening works for you? Tomorrow evening? Sounds perfect."

After finalizing their dinner plans, he remained sitting, staring out the balcony doors where the treetops met the railings of his large terrace.

His latest assignment had been a success and the payment's balance had been placed into his account. But the fact that everything hadn't gone perfectly continued to gnaw at him. He repeatedly replayed the killing in Calgary. He had felt ready with his stance, his gun, his line of sight, his exit plan. But the more he thought about that fleeting moment when the target had looked his way, the more haunted he became about the possibility of his own sloppiness. Perhaps he *had* made a noise. But surely he'd been just as agile and careful as he had been through all his other assignments over the previous two years?

He didn't want to consider the thought that he was no longer excellent at his job. He had to remain excellent. That was what set him above everyone else.

• • •

The next morning, Brielle stepped out of the depths of the Paris metro at Les Halles. She preferred taking taxis, but she had several stops to make and sometimes the metro could be more efficient and less complicated. She'd had to endure the smells of the metro, the worst one being urine, but the trains themselves were clean and well-maintained. And taking one always ensured she got in a bit of a walk.

As usual she had dressed in fine clothes, looking every bit the fashionable French woman, from the ivory clip in her silver hair to her immaculate shoes. And in between? Her stunning and sophisticated navy pantsuit.

She had a busy day ahead before returning home to meet up with her son for dinner. She hadn't seen Jean-Paul in almost two months and looked forward to her time with him.

Her concern for her son had grown since he'd switched jobs two years ago. For the longest time, Jean-Paul's life had seemed stable. She remembered how excited he had been when he'd earned his first job in architecture. That excitement had faded over the years, but that was to be expected. That was real life. That's how things went.

Then he'd told her that although he would always appreciate fine architecture, it was time for a change. His new job in marketing was interesting and paid better, which made up for all the meetings and travelling he now had to endure.

Not only had Jean-Paul's job changed, but he himself had changed. His life had become such a mystery. He was secretive, and Brielle didn't like it. She felt nervous about him and worried that something, somewhere, would soon break. He never seemed relaxed, but always a bit on edge, as if he'd need to leave at any moment to do something.

And his phone never left his side.

After each encounter with Jean Paul, Brielle had made subtle and unsuccessful attempts to learn more about his work. He claimed that he dealt with the ups and downs of the market, and their effects upon large global companies. There were conferences to attend, clients to visit, marketing research to conduct, and industry trends and technology to keep up with. All this involved travel to different cities, mostly in Europe, but some in North America.

When back in Paris, he took Brielle to wonderful Michelin-starred restaurants. He also arranged to take her to shows, plays, and exhibitions. She had no complaints about the financial aspects of his job.

He also regularly deposited money into her bank account, although Brielle, now seventy-seven and retired, didn't need the extra money. Her decades as an administrator in the fashion industry had paid well. She had worked hard and could live comfortably, maintaining the high standard she desired.

But Jean-Paul insisted on giving her what she did not need. To Brielle, it was as if he didn't know what to do with all his money.

Brielle made her way toward Rue Coquillière to carry out a few errands before meeting her friend Marie for lunch. Nearing noon, she entered the restaurant and immediately spotted Marie with her short, spikey white hair and oversized, black-rimmed glasses.

The friends of three decades hadn't had lunch together in over a month, which meant they had much to talk about. With the fashion world surrounding them and more than one hundred museums in the city, they had much to discuss. And they had yet to argue over the growing problem of public vandalism on Paris's streets.

After enjoying a mushroom crepe, Brielle waited for the waiter to finish positioning their coffees in front of them. She then launched into a discussion of Jean-Paul, noting that Marie's shoulders slumped. Brielle ignored the sign, not letting it stop her from expressing her concern.

"Well, I worry about him, Marie. He's been at this marketing job for two years now and I still can't picture what he does. It's not as if he's a lawyer addressing a jury, or a doctor gowned and ready to operate. I can only picture him sitting on a plane or talking on his phone. But he says he's making good money. And did I tell you he's moved into a much larger apartment? He has yet to invite me over. And you know how I had a key to his last apartment? Well, yes, he's given me one to his new place, but he's never asked me to check on the apartment when he's away or collect his mail. Yet he's away so much. I don't understand it. The worst part is that he doesn't seem to be the same person."

After discussing Jean-Paul, as well as the styles of winter coats, the friends went their separate ways.

Brielle walked back toward the Les Halles metro to return home. Before descending the stairs, she glanced left to Église Saint Eustace. Scaffolding, bulldozers, and construction workers in neon vests had interfered with the church's imposing presence for more than a year, but the building now stood free of all those distractions, still imposing but now approachable.

Without further thought, she veered left and followed the curved sidewalk past the shrubbery to the entrance.

Once inside she paused to let her eyes adjust. After making the sign of the cross, she proceeded along the nave, passing rows and rows of empty wooden chairs and occasionally stopping to investigate the intriguing side chapels.

Eventually she approached the altar, the smell of burning candles wafting over her. She stood still and craned her neck toward the silent, glistening organ pipes.

Then she lowered her gaze to a crucifix.

Brielle was no stranger to church, having been raised Catholic. She had tried to raise Jean-Paul in those same traditions, but everything had fallen apart after his father deserted them for a life of less responsibility. Jean-Paul's interest in church had waned when he entered his teen years. Instead of fighting it, Brielle had allowed her own church connection to follow suit; these old churches had now become places to enjoy music, opera, and other performances. She still loved the ambiance of such buildings with their looming statues, ornate altars, and many paintings and sculptures. The stillness invited her into contemplation.

Near the altar, she chose one of the hundreds of wooden chairs and sat. She wasn't alone in the massive stone structure, though. She heard a distant door closing, followed by the sound of footsteps and the muffled voices of visitors strolling the aisles.

Before her, an array of lit candles glimmered in the relative darkness. As she gazed over the flickering flames, her thoughts turned to Saint Eustace. She had lived in Paris all her life and loved the city's history. Even now, the historical facts of Église Saint Eustace remained as clear as ever. Saint Eustace had had a vision in the second century. While hunting, he'd stopped short of killing a deer upon seeing a crucifix in its horns. This vision had led to his conversion. Afterward he had been martyred for refusing to deny his newfound faith. Thus he'd become the patron saint of hunters.

Brielle couldn't help but make a comparison. Years ago, Jean-Paul had taken to the rifle range as a recreational outlet. She had never seen the sense in it, unable to understand his interest. He had never been a hunter. So what was he hunting for in his life?

She felt like praying, something she rarely did—specifically, for Jean-Paul. For his life, his future, his well-being, his happiness. Looking up at the crucifix, she wondered how something so lifeless could help her. She didn't want a statue; she wanted a living God.

She believed in the resurrection of Christ and in the Trinity. It had always made sense to her. But she wondered whether such a God was personally interested in her life. Perhaps not.

Feeling desperate, though, she wondered what harm could come from praying for her son. God might hear her. He might even answer.

She rose and chose a little candle from the table to her left, tilting it to catch the flame of one already lit. She placed it next to the others, then returned to her seat and prayed a short, simple prayer: "God, please help my son."

After watching the flame a moment longer, Brielle stood and made her way back toward the doors, passing a moody painting hanging in a side chapel. She considered how the sombre oil painting was just like Jean-Paul's life—dark but priceless.

* * *

Brielle met Jean-Paul at a restaurant she had never been to, not far from Place Vendôme. In the entryway, mother and son embraced each other. She then stepped back, still holding his hands tight. She wanted some distance to evaluate him.

"*Tu es magnifique*," he remarked.

Brielle wished she could say the same, but Jean-Paul did not look magnificent. He looked pale. She caught the scent of his woody cologne, exuding crisp elegance. At least that reflected some positive impression. And his clothes, of course, were as impeccable as always.

They enjoyed the restaurant's veal sweetbreads with spinach, good enough to convince Brielle that the establishment certainly deserved its Michelin star. Their conversation flowed easily with topics ranging from French politics to the latest books, films, and current museum exhibitions. She always had so much to chat about with Jean-Paul.

While delving into a dessert of pear and black truffles, Brielle decided to ask a more pointed question.

"You've just returned from a market meeting, or a conference?"

"*Oui*. Western Canada this time."

Jean-Paul went on to describe the city of Calgary, how calm, dull, windy, and sunny it was. He spoke of the interesting architecture and showed her a few photos he had taken for her benefit. Perhaps he hoped these details would divert her from asking after his work.

She often tried to visualize the places he chatted about, realizing she had a hard time imagining any setting other than Paris. She sensed he was quieter than normal, though, and wondered whether his work was going as well as it had been.

"Your employment with this company is still good?" she propped. "Profitable, *n'est-ce pas*? You find the work fulfilling?"

His answers may have satisfied others, but not his mother. She sensed that he was avoiding the truth. He quickly changed the subject to discuss some upcoming concerts, hoping they could attend one together in the coming weeks.

After dessert, Brielle felt restless. Jean-Paul was off to meet up with friends—at least, that's what he claimed as they stood outside the restaurant in the pleasant cool air, lanterns highlighting the greenery all around them.

When Brielle's taxi arrived, they hugged goodbye. She wrapped her arms around her son, feeling certain that he had lost some weight. He was already slim and didn't need to lose any more.

In the taxi, Brielle stared out at the passing streetlights, then to the shining Arc de Triomphe, its lights having transformed the monument's grey stone to a brilliant gold. She felt good about having prayed for her son, despite her words to God being few. She decided then and there to make it a practice of stepping into churches to pray as she went about her days. It would be a way to show God that she really was seeking help for her son, and perhaps God might answer.

FIVE

Calgary

ON THE DAY of Aunt Peggy's funeral, Hazel rose early. With hands on hips, she contemplated her open wardrobe. She didn't want to wear the black and taupe ensemble she had worn to Julie's funeral. Her hands slid hangers back and forth until she chose black pants and a black blazer with a white shirt. Once dressed, she concluded that she looked too much like a waiter and switched to a pastel pink blouse.

Because the funeral started at eleven in the morning, Mr. Lee had suggested the day before that Hazel need not bother coming into the office.

"Take the day off, Hazel. You never call in sick anyway. And with the busyness of year-end, you could probably use a break."

Hazel appreciated his words. Despite the year-end financials demanding more of her time, though, she certainly didn't need a break.

She left her apartment, taking the elevator down, and set out for the funeral. Deep in the southeast quadrant of the city, after pulling over twice to check her map, she arrived at the church in frustration. The large parking lot had almost filled up, save for a few empty spots at the far corner. She hurried to the doors, thankful for the pleasant September day that allowed the doors to be propped open. Her breathlessness reminded her of the ten pounds she'd gained over the past decade. Not a lot, but she felt the extra weight and it bothered her. Her good sense of style helped hide her little bulges here and there. It seemed a less painful solution than going to the gym.

Sombre organ music accompanied Hazel's walk down the aisle toward the closed casket. Glad to have spotted the pew her sister sat in, she approached Fran, startling her with a soft tap on the shoulder. Before Fran could show her annoyance, Hazel slid in beside her, forcing Fran to shuffle down.

Hazel leaned forward and stretched her arm across Fran to tap Roger, her brother-in-law, on the arm and flutter a wave further down to their son, Ben. Both men responded with friendly smiles.

Once settled, Hazel's head bobbed around, checking out the other guests and wondering who they all were. There must have been about eighty of them. She sensed the annoyance of her sister, who pointed down to the obituary pamphlet Hazel held.

Hazel responded with a sigh. Always such a good time with Fran. Although the sisters were in their mid-fifties, anyone watching their interactions would conclude they had yet to get past their childhoods.

Before opening the pamphlet, Hazel noticed her sister's midriff and smiled. Sure, Fran was taller and richer. She'd never had to work, not with Roger's income. And sure, she had the bigger house, more expensive jewellery.

But she was also heavier.

Ha! She could stand to lose twenty pounds, and me only ten. Nice to see the tables turning a little bit.

The answer to her question about who all these people were soon became clear when she read the obituary. Aunt Peggy had been involved with Meals on Wheels, Community Kitchen, Inter-City Mission of Hope, and Haiti Relief.

Her reading was interrupted when the organ music abruptly changed to a new but equally sombre hymn. Interspersed between hymns and prayers, friends approached the microphone and spoke about Peggy's contributions to their lives. As Hazel listened to these tales of her aunt's active life, she felt pangs of guilt and a sense of loss.

Why didn't I bother to keep in touch with her? Hazel asked herself. *She was a Mother Teresa and I never even knew it.*

It seemed these ministries were greatly affected in Aunt Peggy's absence. Why did good people have to die when the world needed them?

And then her thoughts turned toward Julie.

Why does God allow these deaths to happen? Aunt Peggy at eighty-five isn't a complete surprise, but Julie... only fifty-four? If anyone had to die, it should have been me. The world would be fine without me. I'm not a fearless leader, an initiator, or a mom.

Julie was still on Hazel's mind as her thoughts turned to Heather, Julie's daughter. Heather had stayed in Calgary for some time, sorting out her mother's estate. Hazel had offered to lend a hand many times, but none had ever been needed. Within a month, Julie's house and contents had been sold. After the celebration of life service, Heather had left for Edmonton with her mother's ashes. And that was that.

When the service for Aunt Peggy ended, she joined Fran and her family to go find their cousin, David. Together they milled around with the other guests, eating crustless egg salad sandwiches very similar to the ones Hazel had imagined. Fran brought David up to date about the family—including her new position as community committee chair, Roger's retirement from the oil and gas business, and Ben's job in computer technology.

The pastor, making his rounds, came by at one point, giving David the opportunity to introduce them all. The pastor smiled as he vigorously shook each of their hands in turn.

As Fran expounded to him every twig of their family tree, Hazel marvelled at her sister's ability to be so abrupt with certain people, such as herself, yet so verbose with others. From time to time, Hazel tried to add a touch of humour, but her quips never landed. Meanwhile, Roger and Ben knew better than to interrupt at all.

When Fran's monologue dwindled, the pastor excused himself to catch up with other parishioners. Hazel thought he looked relieved to escape them.

The fellowship room began to thin out and the three cousins made their goodbyes. They gave each other updated cellphone numbers and emails and promised to keep in touch, maybe for a barbecue.

They exchanged words, but never hugs. Hugs would have been awkward. Hazel wondered whether they would ever show more affection in their greetings and departures.

Hazel began her journey to the far corner of the parking lot, smiling at the conversation she overheard behind her.

"Why do you guys do that?" Ben was asking his mother.

"Do what?"

"Say things like 'We'll have to get together soon for a barbeque.' We never do. Other than Christmas, we never get together with Aunt Hazel."

"Well, we're not saying we'll actually get together. It's just a nice thing to say, even though we probably won't get together till Christmas. Now I need to get going…"

Hazel drove home, relieved that the funeral was over. She agreed with her sister that they would never get together for that barbeque. She didn't even want to see Fran until Christmas, with the usual turkey dinner served at her palace of a house.

At a red light, Hazel wondered why they weren't close. Other sisters got along great and even enjoyed each other's company, despite being different in so many ways. Why couldn't she and Fran manage that?

She crossed the bridge spanning the Bow River and took her usual route onto Fourth Street. The next light glowed green—the start of a green, not a green about to turn yellow. She approached the moderately busy intersection and proceeded through.

As she reached the middle of the intersection, the world around her morphed into slow motion. From her peripheral vision, she glimpsed a half-ton truck, the colour of rusted turquoise, barrelling toward her from the left. It roared through the intersection directly in front of her, coming within less than half a metre.

Shaken, Hazel did the only thing she could—keep going.

Only once she'd gotten through the intersection did she search for a place to pull over. She needed a moment to catch her breath.

Hazel shifted the car into park and allowed her body to tremble. She almost came to tears.

That could've been the end, she realized. *I could've died. I was just inches from death… almost killed while driving home from a funeral.*

She took a few deep breaths.

But I wasn't hit. I wasn't killed. I'm still here.

She sat for another moment, still sorting out exactly what had happened and why.

Who was that idiot anyway? He should be taken off the road and jailed for life.

After taking enough time to settle her mind and body, there was nothing left to do but proceed home. No one had been injured. No vehicles had been damaged. Traffic continued to flow. It seemed as though nothing had happened.

And yet something had.

SIX

Calgary

THE NEXT COUPLE of days at work challenged Hazel more than usual and she didn't know why, except that she couldn't stop thinking about the near miss with that truck. She just couldn't seem to concentrate. The accounts wouldn't quickly balance. She drank coffee after coffee, but it didn't help her figure things out.

Must be a data entry error, she thought, peering at her spreadsheet in confusion and frustration. *But where?*

On Friday, Maddie, knowing Hazel had been bothered by something the entire day, stopped at her doorway at 4:55 p.m.

"Got any plans for the weekend?" Maddie asked.

"No, not really. I'll probably finish my book—a crime thriller, quite good. Should be nice weather, so I'll probably get a walk in. How about you?"

"I'm meeting up with friends tonight to try out a few nightclubs. And, oh yeah, on Sunday my boyfriend and I are heading up to Canmore for a bit of hiking. Always like to get out to the mountains. Well, see ya Monday."

Maddie left.

Left alone, Hazel sat and looked through her office door, thinking about her upcoming weekend. And she thought hard about Maddie's words concerning her plan to get out to the mountains.

Hazel loved the Canadian Rockies, stretching for more than a thousand kilometres and showcasing their stunning beauty to all who were fortunate enough to be in their presence.

She thought back to a certain spring day in April when she'd been in the mountains. The weather had been perfect. No wind at all. She remembered walking a trail and often peering up at the jagged shale and limestone peaks thrusting into the sky. Then she lowered her gaze, following the layers of bare rock till they ended at the treeline. There, dark evergreens took over, blanketing the slopes all the way to the bottom of the valley. And at all sides of the trail, her eyes feasted on wildflowers; she thought some were wild bergamot and purple prairie clover, but she would have needed her *Wildflowers of Alberta* book to confirm. The flowers dotting the scene were endless shades of red, yellow, and purple. Could a day be any more perfect?

Julie had gone on and on, as if their group of five women were climbing Everest. Hazel could still hear Julie shouting "Onward, ladies!" as they took to the lake-hugging gravel trail at Quarry Lake near Canmore.

Those were among her last memories with Julie, although of course she hadn't known it at the time.

At five o'clock, Hazel packed up her desk for the weekend. She re-read Aesop's words from the desk calendar: "Adventure is worthwhile." The words seemed to mock her, emphasizing just how unadventurous her life had become. She imagined the fun Maddie would have dancing and hiking. It wasn't that she felt envious, wanting to go and do likewise; it's just that she dreaded walking out the office door into the void of everyday life.

On the bus, Hazel watched the buildings go by and wished her life was different. How could she change things?

She got off the bus, feeling angry. She suddenly felt like doing something different, even daring. Maybe even something radical.

And so she did.

Hazel made her way to the nearest fast-food outlet, denying herself nothing. Back home, she sat in front of the television and feasted on hamburgers, fries, onion rings, and a chocolate milk-shake while watching the news. While gorging, she heard updates on the fires, floods, and famines around the world.

Once her meal had been polished off, leaving only a small pile of cold fries and a sad third of a hamburger with drooping lettuce, she felt stuffed and unwell. The sense of fun for having indulged in such an unhealthy supper had long passed.

While tossing the leftovers into the compost bin, she heard a favourite song from the 1980s accompanying a television commercial. She returned to her living room just in time to catch the end of the ad, featuring a truck that sped down roads, spitting dust in its wake. It stopped on a ridge, where a family of three emerged to enjoy the mountain view and set up camp under the setting sun.

Hazel felt anything but inspired to buy that truck or any other. She wondered how much gas had been burned, how much high alpine terrain had been destroyed to reach such a lofty height.

But one word from the commercial struck Hazel— *adventure.* Everyone was out and about seeking adventure.

Adventure is always worthwhile.

She walked over to her balcony and stepped outside. Once again, the wind was picking up leaves and swirling them around. Could the wind pick her up and blow her away to a better life?

Surprised at the question, she felt restless and unanchored.

A leaf hit Hazel on the cheek, bringing her back to her reality. This wasn't getting her anywhere. The answers to her problems weren't blowin' in the wind.

Back inside, she sat in front of the television. She attributed her sense of lostness to Julie's death. Since then her life had shrunk and could be described with unflattering words like *boring, uneventful,* and *unimportant.* Her life lacked purpose and fun.

Lacklustre. That was a good word for it.

She thought of Aunt Peggy and the vibrant life she'd lived. Everyone was going to miss her. All those ministries would notice.

No one would miss me much if I died in a car accident, she thought. *I can see my tombstone now: "Other than keeping accounts balanced, most of the time, she had little effect upon the world."*

But Aunt Peggy? Julie? They were missed.

As Hazel contemplated her life, she detected a tiny ray of hope. Her life had been spared from that madman in the turquoise truck, so her life must have some significance. A little bit anyway. Obviously this was not yet her time to die. God still had a reason for her to be here, although she couldn't imagine what it might be.

Her theology told her that God would never desert her, that he was always by her side. She thought of Jesus's words from somewhere in Hebrews about never leaving nor forsaking his children. She could also spout off Philippians 4:6–7 flawlessly and she chose this moment to say the words aloud.

"Do not be anxious about anything, but in every situation, by prayer and petition, with thanksgiving, present your requests to God. And the peace of God, which transcends all understanding, will guard your hearts and your minds in Christ Jesus."

Now her theology was being tested by experience. She had to believe that God would never desert her. Her prayers had a purpose. Otherwise why would Jesus have taught his disciples to pray? She knew that prayer should be her automatic response to times in life that felt overwhelming. But seldom did she see any difference after praying.

Maybe I'm not looking hard enough for answers. Maybe my prayers aren't specific enough. Maybe I want God's answers to be spectacular, except they're ordinary. I don't know.

Soft tears made their way down Hazel's cheeks, falling to the point of her chin. She allowed them to continue for several minutes before grabbing a tissue to dry her eyes, cheeks, and chin, and to blow her nose.

Leaning forward with slumped shoulders, she cleared her throat. Only a whisper came out. She didn't concern herself with the volume, for she believed that God had perfect hearing. He could hear her voice, her pain, her heartfelt longings.

"God, I need your help. So much in my life feels so… so empty. It's empty yet heavy—a weird, empty heaviness. I think I've lost my purpose. My focus. And that's why I feel out of sorts and depressed so much of the time. I don't do much of anything anymore. Not since you took Julie. But you had your reasons for taking her, and I admit that I don't understand them. I need to realize that it's okay not to understand. You don't expect me to. Anyway, what I want to say is that I'm not content with my life. I'm not motivated to do anything meaningful, adventurous, or fun. I feel alone. I feel useless at church. I feel hurt and angry all the time with Fran…"

At the thought of Fran, Hazel's mind drifted, becoming fixated on their relationship. Their lack of closeness frustrated her, and the age difference hadn't helped. Having three years between them meant that when Hazel had entered junior high, Fran had already been off to high school. And when Hazel entered grade ten, Fran was off to university. Their paths seemed only to intersect when necessary.

And yet there had been a time, eons ago, when things were good. This had been particularly true in their preteen years, travelling with their parents, usually into neighbouring British Columbia. For two weeks every summer, their mutual confinement in the family car had developed in them a sense of camaraderie. Spending seven hours together in the car meant they might as well get along and play games like travel bingo. And upon arriving in the Okanagan, they might as well play frisbee on the beach, then jump from their air mattresses into the lake, splashing each other.

Those had been good days. But they were so few.

"Lord, I don't know what to do. I'm so unhappy. Help me with Fran. Lead me to your joy, to the things that matter in this life, to what you want me to do and the people you want me to help. Show me how to be effective and involved in life. Help me not feel so afraid of what or who might be taken away from me next. Help me not to be scared of the future."

She felt a little lighter. She didn't want to question whether God would help but chose to consider how it would be done. What would he do? Would she recognize his work in her life? Her prayer requests were all over the map.

The smell of deep-fried food hung in the air and she raised her hand to her stomach. Indigestion and heartburn had built up. Why had she chosen to eat such food? She usually ate better than this. What a stupid adventure that had been!

Remembering the receipt she had found on the bus a week ago, her thoughts turned to that French restaurant. Although rich, that food must surely be healthier. She worked to recall every detail of that stranger's lavish dinner.

She opened her laptop to research every French restaurant in Calgary and smiled when she encountered the one from the receipt: La Vie en Ville, which she soon discovered meant "the city of life." Their website included a menu written in an elegant font, listing entrées with English translations. The photos revealed exquisite plates of food and the room looked so warm and inviting.

Who had the stranger been? Her imagination insisted that it must have been a woman, and probably a wealthy woman. Maybe an older widow having a night out. Maybe she was finally getting over the death of her dearly loved husband and readying herself to start living again. Well, good for her.

Hazel pictured the widow dressed in richly coloured fabrics. Silk. Linen. And in a deep burgundy… no, maybe green. A soft, muted, medium-dark green. She'd have worn a kind of wrap around her shoulders. She'd be comfortable, confident, and at ease with her surroundings.

Hazel tried to remember what else the person had ordered besides the beef. There had been a long word beginning with *vissy*. Hazel researched this and brought up a picture of a cold potato soup called *vichyssoise*. She remembered the third item on the receipt had been a drink, something alcoholic. Hazel wasn't much of a wine drinker—for that matter, she hardly partook of any alcohol. A half-glass of wine at a special occasion would last her the entire evening.

She didn't remember the exact cost of the meal, either. From the online menu, she added up the price and decided that it must be a spectacular waste of money.

But then she closed her eyes and heard Julie's voice whispering right into her ear: *"Why not?"*

Hazel grabbed the phone.

"Hello, I'd like to make a reservation for one person tomorrow evening around 6:00?" she said when a woman answered. "Oh, that's wonderful! It's Hazel... H-A-Z-E-L. Yes, that's right. My last name?"

Oh, for Pete's sake, you're a small restaurant. Do you really need my last name?

"Sommerville," she said at last. "Hazel Sommerville. Okay. Thank you."

Hazel abandoned the television. She entered the bedroom and once again stood in front of her open closet, contemplating what she might wear for the occasion. Dresses, skirts, and pants soon piled up on her bed, a pile topped with flung scarves. As Hazel whittled the pile to a few choice outfits, a feeling of excitement grew inside her. A feeling she hadn't felt in a long time. She sensed God leading her into adventure—perhaps a small adventure, but an adventure nonetheless.

SEVEN

Calgary

HAZEL DROVE DOWNTOWN and across the river, tackling many one-way avenues before arriving at a parkade close to La Vie en Ville. She quickened her steps in the chilly autumn air and jaywalked. Anyone watching her might think she was talking to someone via Bluetooth rather than practicing the pronunciation of French foods.

Once inside, the entry greeted Hazel with a lovely warmth. She took in the small round tables draped in white linen, half of which looked occupied. She detected the smell of what might have been steak, not overpowering but enticing.

A desperately thin hostess approached Hazel and smiled. "*Bon soir, madame.* Do you have a reservation with us this evening?"

"Yes, I do. For Hazel Sommerville, six o'clock."

Her eye scrolled down the paper in a black folder. "*Ah, oui.* This way please."

She led Hazel to a table midway along the restaurant's redbrick wall. She informed Hazel that Leon would be her waiter for the evening.

While waiting for Leon, Hazel took off her coat and didn't know what to do with it. Other customers didn't seem to have coats lying about, so maybe she'd missed a coatrack. Telling herself to relax, Hazel neatly folded her coat and laid it with her purse out of sight on the opposite chair.

Why am I nervous? You'd think I'd never been to a restaurant before. Maybe it's just the awkwardness of dining alone. Or maybe it's being in such a lovely restaurant.

Without a window nearby to peer through, she glanced around the restaurant feeling like a spy. Each table had a single flower in a petite crystal vase; some held carnations and others held roses. She admired the rose before her and considered it a sign.

A rose for Hazel Rose Sommerville. Maybe this is where I'm supposed to be right now at this very moment.

She smiled at the thought, knowing the chances of getting a rose at her table would have been fifty-fifty. She wasn't convinced it signified a divine confirmation. Why would God care where she was eating right now? And why would he care which flower decorated her table?

She took note of what the other women were wearing. Despite her fish-out-of-water feelings, she felt she had dressed appropriately in her green silk blouse and burgundy scarf.

One senior couple caught her attention. He was as handsome as she was stunning, perfect candidates to advertise a cruise line. Hazel imagined them leaning against a ship's railing, flashing their perfect teeth, laughing and pointing to something ashore. She watched the woman drink her wine; after taking a sip, her fingers remained curled around the glass's stem. Hazel herself had nothing to drink and so busied her hands adjusting her scarf.

Only when she stopped fussing did she notice the soft jazz in the background. It wasn't Édith Piaf, but it was still lovely. She took a deep breath and tried to let her body slow down and connect with the music.

A teenage-looking Leon arrived, dressed smartly in black and white with a bowtie. He introduced himself, handed Hazel a menu, and poured cold water with ice into her glass.

"Have you decided what you'd like to drink this evening? We have a lovely Burgundy Chablis."

Hazel had prepared herself. "I'll be fine with the water. Thank you."

Leon walked away, perhaps disappointed. Hazel couldn't tell.

When he returned, he announced: "This evening, we have the salmon seasoned with lemon and rosemary, set over a bed of green beans and sided with asparagus and carrots."

"Thank you, but I think I'll have the *vee-shee-swaz* please, and the *beef brogan no*. Thank you."

"Very well, madame."

Leon left and Hazel felt proud of her pronunciation.

She thought about the receipt stranger. Believing that the woman had dined alone helped her to feel better about her own situation. But who had she been, really? What was she like?

Hazel imagined sitting and dining with the stranger. They'd chat about how their days had gone, about what they'd done, and what dreams they held for the future. Because of the odd little connection she had with this person, she even silently prayed for her. Hazel prayed that if the woman didn't have faith in God, didn't have a clue who Christ was, she might one day come to know him personally.

The *vichyssoise* arrived. Hazel enjoyed the cold leek and potato soup but believed a little heat would have improved it. She smiled, picturing a French chef's face aghast at being asked to zap her soup.

Hazel loved the boeuf bourguignon, though, finding it to be as substantial as a rich, hearty stew.

Leon came back around afterward and cleared her table. He then returned with a dessert menu, which provided a choice of three items. Hazel envisioned herself sipping a hot decaf coffee between dainty forkfuls of tiramisu.

But the receipt woman hadn't ordered dessert or coffee. And why not? It would have been wonderful to munch on a sweet dessert right now.

I love tiramisu and can't remember the last time I had it. There's nothing stopping me from ordering it now.

Oddly, it didn't feel right, as if doing such a thing would dishonour the receipt itself—or worse, dishonour the receipt woman.

"I'm sorry, but I can't… I mean, I'm rather full. Thank you. It was very delicious."

Leon left and Hazel stared blankly at the melting ice cubes at the bottom of her empty water glass. Suddenly she imagined a pair of figures, one perched on each of her shoulders. It seemed impossible to distinguish which one represented the devil and which one an angel.

"Why not have dessert, Hazel? Nothing wrong with that. Who says you're obligated to follow a little piece of paper?"

The other voice was quick to counter, "Hazel, great job! You followed through. You don't need all that sugar anyway."

When the bill arrived, she hesitated. Had the woman paid with a credit card or cash? How much had she tipped? Oh, for Pete's sake just pay the silly thing.

Leon returned and handed Hazel the machine to insert her credit card. She gave a twenty-percent tip and waited for the receipt, which she tucked in her purse, not wanting to be as careless as the original stranger who'd dined here.

Back in her car, driving home, Hazel pushed aside the confusion and silliness of having taken the receipt so seriously. She knew that a little piece of paper was just a piece of paper. It wasn't like the receipt was the inspired Word of God. She chuckled and acknowledged, though, that she felt elated. She'd just had an adventure!

Once home and changed into sweatpants and a T-shirt, Hazel plunked herself down on the couch to catch up on the Saturday evening news, all the while enjoying a dish of chocolate ice cream with vanilla wafer cookies on the side.

EIGHT

Calgary

HAZEL TOOK HER usual back pew and listened to the morning announcements. The pleas for volunteers to help in Sunday school, set out refreshments, and count the offering money sounded desperate. Hazel dismissed each one. She sat in her church-spectator frame of mind, having forgotten her prayer two nights ago for God to change her life.

Now that summer was over, the pastor began a new sermon series. Its subject was prayer, although Hazel had been unaware of this due to losing interest in upcoming church events and failing to keep herself informed. The church emails she received went straight into the trash folder.

But she sat up straighter when he began to speak. A prayer series was exactly what she needed.

The pastor encouraged the congregants to examine their current prayer lives. He then suggested that they start prayer journals.

"Writing things down often helps you see things clearly," he said. "Even if you only keep a journal for one week, it helps. Be aware of when you pray and what you pray for. Are your prayers general or specific? How much of your prayer revolves around informing God of what's going on? Remember, he needs no informing. By taking a good look at your prayer lives, I hope you will see areas in need of change and improvement."

He proceeded to introduce some principles he'd be exploring over the next several weeks: how to incorporate scripture into one's prayers, how God answers in ways never expected, how people are often involved in the answering of prayers, and how prayer is ultimately a reflection of one's relationship with God.

After the benediction, Hazel hung around. She wasn't sure why. Somehow it didn't seem right to rush away. Perhaps subconsciously, she recalled the phrases she had uttered to God: "I feel useless." "Lead me to the things that matter." "Help me be effective and involved in life."

Perhaps she enjoyed the sermon and was in a good mood, or perhaps it was the enticing aroma of the coffee being served nearby.

Hazel noticed a familiar couple on refreshment duty that morning. Brent and Stacy sure knew how to make a good cup of coffee. Decent. Strong. None of that dishwater stuff. She poured herself a cup and stood to the side, taking in the chatter but otherwise remaining invisible.

"Hazel!"

She looked up to spot Gloria heading towards her like a wasp ready to sting. Just like that, Hazel knew she had made a mistake by sticking around. Watching Gloria could be so exhausting. In her late thirties, with three preteen children, Gloria had her hands full. But somehow her short, thin frame never ran out of energy she needed to handle her family, nor the happenings within the church family. Hazel saw her as a friendly and committed Christian woman. Not a busybody, but definitely busy.

"If you have a minute, I'd like to talk with you," Gloria said, coming right up to her and making no attempt to discover whether Hazel truly had a minute or not.

Hazel braced herself for what would no doubt be a request.

"Now, I know how good you are with finances. Everyone knows that! At this point, we need people to count the offering money. I don't think we've ever had so few people to help out. Several have moved away. The Strands to Victoria, and the Taylors—well, they haven't moved away but are gone for a few months. I know you've helped out a lot in the past, but not lately. And the situation we're in, well… it's just difficult for the same people to always stay after church to do this. We really do need help."

Gloria didn't mention Julie, who had been the head church teller for years. Everyone at the church knew that Hazel felt her friend's loss more deeply than most in the congregation.

"Dealing with the offering money on Sundays keeps getting easier, with more tithes coming in as e-transfers, but still there are cheques and cash to account for," Gloria continued. "Think about it and let me know. Of course, this wouldn't be every Sunday, maybe just once a month. You used to do it so well, and fast. Anyway, get back to me when you can. Have a good week!"

Gloria left to chat with other people, leaving Hazel to down her coffee before anyone else could approach her about helping in Sunday school.

She drove home while anticipating the start of her prayer journal. As soon as she'd heard the pastor mention the idea in his sermon, she had known it was for her. Anything to do with pen, paper, and writing must be beneficial.

Once home, she squatted down to glance at a few empty journals on her bookcase's bottom shelf. With a touch of excitement, she grabbed one. The one with the turquoise cover, in honour of the truck that had failed to kill her.

I'm still here and I have things to write about. Things to pray about.

That afternoon, she sat at the table, journal open and pen in hand, remembering the morning sermon. Life seemed a little brighter since the previous day's prayer. And now she believed things would become even brighter, clearer, more organized.

She divided a page into two columns, the first column for prayer requests and the second for the answers.

Let's see, she thought. *I want to be adventurous, like I was when Julie was alive. I want fun back in my life. I want to be like Aunt Peggy—doing things, helping people. Things that matter. But I don't want to be like Fran, overextending myself as I run everything.*

The thought of Fran hit Hazel with sadness. Well, sadness and sarcasm.

I really, really need to pray about my relationship with Fran. God still works miracles, doesn't he?

Hazel felt like she was drumming up a shopping list for God. *Specifics. I need specifics.*

She tried to give each request a similar grammatical structure so the words flowed, but she couldn't. Eventually she summarized her words into three requests:

1. Be adventurous
2. Be helpful
3. Have a better relationship with Fran

Hazel wanted God to know that she was serious, that she anticipated his help. But she couldn't help but wonder about the cost. Everything had a cost. How would her routine and comfort be affected? She didn't want adventure to lead to her demise, like falling from a mountaintop. She didn't want to overcommit herself with good works so she never had time to relax anymore. And she couldn't imagine how her relationship with her sister could ever improve.

She looked at her journal page, determined to transform all that negative white space with meaningful words.

Well, I've prayed about these things. Now I'll see how God leads me... how he answers.

Later that afternoon, Hazel walked the long stretch of the park near her apartment. No picnics were taking place now that the cooler autumn days had arrived. The ball diamond lay empty. But dog-walkers and families on bikes gave motion, energy, and a busyness to the greenspace.

As Hazel walked, leaves crunching underfoot, she thought about Gloria's request. Helping out wouldn't be a heavy burden. In fact, counting the offering money would be simple. It was a task she'd done before. She replayed Gloria's words: "You're so good with numbers." It felt good to be acknowledged, to be wanted and needed.

By the time Hazel returned home, she had made up her mind. She would talk to Gloria next Sunday and watch the woman's face beam with delight. She sat down, picked up her pen, and wrote a few new words in her journal, under the "Be helpful" column: *serving as church teller.*

Throughout the afternoon and evening, another idea percolated in Hazel's mind. It concerned something she could add to the "Fran" column. Or it could turn out to be a disaster.

Before the hour grew too late, Hazel decided to take the plunge and follow through.

This idea is so absurd, she thought. *It must be from God!*

She picked up the phone and called her sister, preparing herself for the short jabs she always received when they talked, not to mention the perhaps long-winded ramblings.

"Hi Fran," Hazel began.

"What's wrong? Is something wrong?"

"No, nothing's wrong. I'm just calling to see if you, Roger, and Ben might be free sometime over the Thanksgiving weekend to come over for dinner. I know that's not for another few weeks but—"

"To your place?"

No, I was thinking of a mountaintop picnic.

"Yes, my place. I'm cooking a turkey with all the trimmings. Is there a night you might be free that weekend?"

Fran hesitated. "You're really going to cook a turkey? Okay… well, let me look at my calendar."

Hazel knew it was all about Fran's schedule, because Roger didn't have one. She waited several minutes before Fran's voice came back over the line.

"I do have several things on the go," her sister said. "Our church is having a Thanksgiving potluck dinner on the Friday. Can you believe it? I thought it rather silly. People are already committed to family gatherings and now we're supposed to meet on Friday? I tried to get that changed, but the others on the committee wanted to go ahead... anyway, let me see what else there is. Saturday is out of the question. And of course Sunday is impossible. I suppose Monday evening could work, as long as it's not a late dinner. I have so much on the go the next day. Anyway. I'm sure Roger is free. Of course I have no idea about Ben, but I'll text you."

"Okay, great. How about if we eat around six? Come by at five-thirty if you'd like."

"Now are you sure you can manage with the three of us there? I mean, your place is so small."

Hazel sighed quietly. "Yes, I can manage it. We'll make it work."

"Then what can I bring? How about an appetizer? A salad? And maybe a dessert?"

Why don't you bring the turkey, stuffing, mashed potatoes, and gravy too, for Pete's sake.

"No, that's fine, Fran. You don't need to bring anything."

"Are you sure? I don't mind. Have you cooked a turkey before?"

Hazel stifled her growing anger. "Of course I've cooked a turkey before."

So what if that was a decade or two ago.

"Well, okay. Text if there's anything I can do. Now what about parking? It's so congested down there. Last time I was over, whenever that was, I had the worst time trying to find a spot. What a nightmare."

"There's visitor parking which usually has several open spots. Then again, I suppose those would be full, it being the Thanksgiving weekend. But there's plenty of street parking. I'm sure you'll find something close."

Fran sighed. "Well, we'll see what we can do."

After the call, Hazel sat on the couch in disbelief. Her Fran Plan was going to happen. Was it a bad idea? No matter what, it would certainly be an adventure. Fran had sure sounded surprised.

Hazel spent the rest of the evening online, researching how to cook a turkey. She also began a list of ingredients she'd need to buy. By the time she went to bed, her list had evolved into a detailed spreadsheet.

NINE

Paris

ON A CRISP day in early October, Brielle arrived in the area of St. German de Prés when she received a text from Marie, indicating she would be half an hour late for lunch. Instead of going into Les Deux Magots to get a table and wait, Brielle crossed the street.

Stonework, brown brick, and a roof of worn grey shingles made up the exterior of St. Germain de Prés; it emitted a charm like no other Parisian church could. Brielle looked up to the window boxes running along the side of the building, showcasing red geraniums. The red blossoms and greenery nestled below each window added a finishing touch, as if their shot of colour had always been meant to be there. Despite the shorter, cooler days of October, they would defy autumn's arrival for as long as possible.

Brielle walked to the dark arched alcove, but a woman robed in black emerged from the darkness before she could open the church door. Her bony hand, like that of an evil witch, reached out as if to grab Brielle's coat. But she didn't grab; instead she held open her empty, skeletal hand, keeping it close to Brielle's face.

Brielle couldn't ignore the woman's stench. Repulsed, she wanted to get away but momentarily didn't know whether to go back out to the street or enter the church. Abruptly she brushed past the woman, grabbing the door handle and proceeding inside.

Once inside, she stopped to collect her thoughts. She needed to rid herself of the image of the woman in ragged black, not to mention the decrepit hand that belonged to a life of dirt and poverty.

She walked along the nave, attempting to concentrate on the beauty of the turquoise pillars topped with gold figurines. But it proved difficult. Her mind refused to let go of the image of the street woman. She wondered what events had transpired in her life to bring her to such a point of desperation.

Brielle noticed a poster advertising Sponsor a Painting, a new campaign underway; she appreciated having something else to think about. She read the details and preferred this approach of asking for money. So much more civilized. She even considered supporting the project, preferring this brand of charity over doling out money to a poor person.

She gazed up at the paintings of Christ around the church. Jesus entering Jerusalem. Jesus riding a donkey. Jesus carrying his cross up to Golgotha. Were some of these paintings in need of a sponsor? They didn't appear to require restoration.

Besides being known as the oldest church in Paris, to Brielle this church would never die. It had been rebuilt after each Viking invasion in the sixth century. Repairs had continued century after century. More recently, during the French Revolution, repairs had been made after an accidental explosion of stored gunpowder. With every reparation, the building had taken on the newest architectural style.

Brielle considered how this history reflected life. People lived for decades, always the same person yet undergoing change to adapt to whatever chaos was thrown their way. People did what they must to survive.

She felt a twinge of surprise at the philosophical bent her mind had taken.

A young couple, possibly tourists, passed by and offered Brielle a respectful smile, something to which she had grown accustomed as a stylish native Parisian. She thought it rather amusing. She maintained her stoic refinement and never smiled back.

At the front of the church, Brielle lit a tea candle and sat for a few moments to pray for her son. Emotion overcame her and she tried unsuccessfully to hold back tears. She felt so annoyed with herself, not only becoming philosophical but now emotional. She knew her concern for Jean-Paul continually built up and she needed to give her worries over to God. Her words to God, although still not many, became more targeted.

"If this is not the job for him, please lead him to something else," she murmured. "I want him to be happy."

With the half-hour now past, Brielle wiped away all evidence of tears and regained her air of sophistication.

She rose from her chair and exited the church, relieved that the street woman had disappeared from the entryway. She walked back toward Les Deux Magots and got a table just when Marie arrived.

Over lunch, Marie commented on Brielle's new haircut with highlights. Brielle commented on Marie's new wool coat. The conversation continued in this manner, covering the latest fashion arrivals at Les Galleries Lafayette.

When the conversation veered away from fashion, Marie talked about her children and grandchildren. Then Brielle steered the discussion toward Jean-Paul, trying to be upbeat. She mentioned their recent restaurant venture.

"And he's looking into getting tickets for the Festival Resonance at La Sainte Chapelle," Brielle added. "I haven't been to that church for a while. It is the most magnificent, isn't it?"

"So he must be in town for a while?"

"Apparently he's here for most of the fall, although I know his schedule can change and suddenly he's off to another city. Another country. He mentioned going to Spain sometime in November. He did seem rather vague."

Marie seemed to immediately detect the weariness Brielle wore on her face. "But you still worry about him, *non?*"

"I worry about him all the time. When we're together, he's distracted. His thoughts pull him away. He's too thin. I don't understand him anymore, Marie. What is he struggling with? It must be his job. I know he was increasingly unhappy with his job as an architect, but he certainly isn't thriving in this new position."

"You know, Brielle, it could be a woman. Love can mess up a person's life like nothing else. However, as you say, it could be his job. Anyway, I have no idea of Jean-Paul's problem. But I was thinking... you say that you have a key to his new apartment, *n'est-ce pas?*"

Brielle hesitated. "*Oui*. He gave me one when he first moved in. Why?"

She regarded her friend with slight amusement, as though waiting to hear of some clandestine plot.

"Perhaps, when you know he is away, you could make a small detour in your day and stop in there," Marie suggested.

"Why would I do that? What would you expect me to find?"

Marie raised her hands in mock exasperation. "*Je ne sais pas.* Perhaps something that tells you his life is going well, that all this worry is unnecessary. Maybe you'll see two empty wineglasses by the sink in his kitchen—okay, he has a girlfriend. That could be good news... or not. You could look around and see that he is taking care of his place. Is he watering his plants? You say he is usually tidy and organized. So is his place tidy and organized? Perhaps you'll see something that encourages you. Perhaps that is all you need. This little exploit might give you positive information. Something."

"Well, he's never owned any plants, not even ones to put out on his terrace—nothing he needs to maintain. Anyway, I have absolutely no idea what I would find that would encourage me. I've mentioned to him that I would love to see his apartment, but he just says that there isn't much to see. It's just in a better location, he says. But what if his plans change and he suddenly arrives home to see me in his apartment?"

The waiter brought their coffees and they both busied themselves stirring in the cream.

"Well, you would go when you know he is far away," Marie said. "In California or somewhere like that."

After a few sips, Brielle said, "I suppose it wouldn't hurt to see what his place looks like. Maybe you're right. It might be encouraging. But I would never, ever want him to know I had been there."

"*Non. Non.* Of course not, Brielle."

* * *

In the early days of autumn, Jean-Paul spent much of his time at rifle ranges, as was his practice. He visited a variety of them, both in Paris and the surrounding area.

He had always enjoyed the rifle range, ever since he and some friends in their late teens had ventured to one on a lazy summer afternoon. He still remembered the hard time his friends had given him—not for being a lousy shot, but for being excellent.

"You should join the Police Nationale," they teased.

He was surprised to have found an ability in which he so quickly excelled. He was a natural.

Jean-Paul also liked to take advantage of using unfamiliar rifles and needed to challenge himself at different ranges to maintain his accuracy. His job required this, for his associates knew he never travelled armed. Jean-Paul always made it clear: "I'll do the job, and I'll do it perfectly. You provide what I need when I arrive at the location." He was too good a marksman for anyone to argue with him.

Whatever range at which he found himself, he felt a measure of peace. He counted on these exercises to keep himself sharp. The appeal was much like getting lost in a well-loved hobby—a hobby that didn't result in killing anyone, at least not at the range. He kept reminding himself of what he had been told: that those he killed deserved to die. They had made themselves a target because of their vile choices. He simply helped people deal with those targets in their lives.

One pleasant evening in Paris, after practicing at the range, Jean-Paul sat alone on a café patio. He faced the unhurried pace of passersby and the rush of cars along the Boulevard de Port-Royal. The autumn breeze felt refreshing. The sound of light rock drifted from the kitchen. Out in public like this, Jean-Paul didn't feel lonely.

He sipped red wine and allowed his thoughts to wander. As he watched an older couple slowly pass, his thoughts circled around to the simple reality that everyone ages. Old age and death terrified him, like an overpowering wave dragging him out to dark waters.

Despite not even being fifty, over the past week he had returned again and again to the idea of retirement—early retirement. No longer did the idea of working for another decade sound appealing. Ten years felt too heavy, with the finish line not even visible on the horizon. Why ten? Why not cut that in half? Five years sounded better. Lighter and doable. He didn't want to continue too long, with these nagging doubts about his sharpness. Five more years of income should suffice.

TEN

Calgary

HAZEL LOOKED TO her office wall calendar. Days earlier, she had flipped the page to reveal a picture of pumpkins piled high in front of a red barn door. She appreciated the warmth of its colours. October had arrived and Evergreen's financial reports had been finalized, completing another year-end. The coming month would be calmer.

While on coffee breaks, she often found herself glancing at her phone's Thanksgiving spreadsheet. She had already purchased nonperishables such as a tin of cranberry sauce and an orange candle for a centrepiece. She'd bought a turkey and managed to shove it into the freezer compartment of her fridge, believing she had suffered only minor frostbite.

When Thanksgiving weekend arrived, Hazel spent her Saturday morning shopping. The supermarket was a blur of shoppers and carts and noise, a reminder of why she usually avoided shopping on Saturdays, especially on a holiday weekend.

Pushing her grocery-laden cart across the parking lot, Hazel forged into the strong west wind. She nudged the cart up against the back of her car and opened the trunk, all the while bodily blocking the cart so it wouldn't take off. She carefully placed each bag, including one that contained a dozen eggs and another with the last of the store's pumpkin pies.

Once behind the wheel, she gave a great sigh. What a wind! That effort had taken every ounce of energy she had left.

Before leaving the parking lot, she retrieved a slip of paper from her pocket. Back in the supermarket, in the produce section, she'd noticed the receipt stuck to the side of the cart. Standing in front of tomatoes and avocados, Hazel had tucked it away in her coat pocket. Now she examined the details.

She hadn't considered that the La Vie en Ville receipt would be the first in a series. It hadn't seemed like the start of something, but now she wasn't so sure.

Hazel clutched this second receipt, acknowledging that it held no power over her. At the same time, she couldn't ignore it. It suggested the continuation of a game. It offered a challenge and seemed to invite her to take a step along an unscripted path.

From the window, she surveyed the concrete terrain between her parking space and the coffee shop across from the grocery store.

Well, why not? she thought, vacillating as she listened to the howls of the wind. *It's right over there, for Pete's sake. Simple enough. I just need to pretend I have the energy.*

As much as she didn't want to open the car door, she didn't want to give in to the wind.

She pushed the door open and held it from slamming back onto her legs. With head bent low, she battled the wind and hurried, wondering why some parking lots were built so unnecessarily massive.

Hazel reached the Cup or Two Café, not a totally unfamiliar place. She'd been here a few times before. Like the supermarket, it too was busy and Hazel had to stand in line for several minutes before her turn to order. She remembered the order from the latest receipt: a large coffee and a donut.

She found an unoccupied table, brushed the few crumbs off the chair, and sat down.

On her second bite of donut, she wondered whose receipt she had retrieved. She imagined a young mother having gone to get groceries for Thanksgiving dinner. She'd probably treated herself to a coffee and donut first. Maybe she had a play-before-work mentality. Not a great work ethic.

To Hazel, it didn't matter whose receipt it was. What mattered was the adventure.

She enjoyed her mid-morning treat while examining her list of things to do in preparation for Monday's dinner. She believed she had all she needed from the store.

Leaving the café, with the wind at her back, she struggled to keep control of her own pace. Frustration built when she couldn't locate her car right away.

"This wind is so… so stupid," she muttered, trying to come up with the most derogatory term imaginable.

Once back in the calm of her apartment, Hazel felt that her unexpected donut detour deserved at least a line or two in her journal, under the "Adventure" heading. As she wrote, she decided to make this a ritual every time she found a receipt. Of course, she knew it would seldom happen.

The next morning in church, Hazel tried to pay attention to the sermon, but her thoughts often drifted back to Thanksgiving dinners of the past. She remembered her mother ruling the kitchen, never wanting help. She'd made the pumpkin pie and cranberry sauce. She'd set the table. And she'd gotten all the praise for having done the work to present a lavish feast for her family, always laying out a scene of perfection. The only opportunity to help would come after the meal, when the table looked like the aftermath of a vulture attack; she and her sister always cleaned up the mess and washed the dishes.

At an early age, Hazel had settled into her place in the world. A place off to the side of the main event. A place to observe and not get in the way. She felt comfortable there. Meanwhile, she watched Fran turn into their mother, with a need to control as much as possible.

Everyone stood for the closing hymn, but Hazel wasn't quite on cue.

After the service, her fellow congregants seemed preoccupied with plans for their own busy days. No one stayed long after the service for coffee, except for a few who likely only lingered because they had no family to visit. It occurred to Hazel that she might reach out next year and invite some of these lonely souls back to her place.

For now she had to focus on Fran and her family's impending visit. That was enough to deal with.

For the balance of the afternoon, Hazel gave her apartment a thorough cleaning.

Early Monday morning, she made the turkey stuffing and gleefully checked other items off her spreadsheet. At noon, she slid the stuffed turkey into the oven. The plan was for everyone to eat at six o'clock.

By four o'clock, the delicious aroma of roasting turkey dominated every room of the nine-hundred-square-foot apartment. Hazel stood out on her balcony and peered down to the front entrance, watching people come and go. The wind had died down considerably and she appreciated the cool autumn air, wondering how the dinner would go and questioning whether this was a good idea. Too late now, of course.

At quarter to six, she opened the door to greet Fran, Roger, and Ben. Fran extended a sack to Hazel, offering no explanation. A peek inside the bag revealed a cheesecake and buns.

"Oh, you didn't need to bring anything," Hazel reminded her.

I told you not to, she seethed. *So unnecessary and annoying. But why listen to me?*

Hazel took the cake and buns and wondered where she could put them amongst everything else already piled high on her counters.

Then Hazel asked a question she immediately regretted. "You found a parking spot okay?"

"Well, yes," said Fran. "Eventually."

Roger managed to interject. "It wasn't that big a deal."

As if Roger hadn't spoken, Fran continued. "As expected, the visitor parking was full. So we drove around and around until we finally found a place way down the street. It's so congested around here."

Hazel had nothing more to add and so got on with being a good hostess. "What can I get everybody to drink?"

After she'd served the beverages, Ben turned to her and smiled. "I like your place, Aunt Hazel."

"Thanks, Ben. It's been a long time since you've been here."

They didn't chat about their last long-ago visit since no one could remember when that was.

When they sat down to eat, Fran did most of the talking, bringing Hazel needlessly up to date with her neighbourhood gossip and church activities. At times Roger and Ben found opportunities to steer the conversation toward more interesting subjects, like movies, books, and even sports.

Everyone seemed to enjoy the meal. Even Fran managed to compliment Hazel.

As Hazel began clearing the dishes to make room for coffee and dessert, Fran stood up and hovered by her chair.

"I'd help you with that, but I don't think two people can fit in your kitchen," Fran said. "How do you manage in such a tiny space?"

Hazel loved her kitchen too much to remain silent. "I know it's not huge, but it's compact and efficient. It works well and I love it."

"Ever thought of moving further out into the suburbs?"

Hazel pretended not to have heard her over the clattering of the dishes.

They were soon indulging in coffee and pumpkin pie, although Hazel also put out Fran's cheesecake. Roger, ever the peacemaker even though he'd eaten too much already, took a piece of both desserts.

The three offered to help Hazel clean up afterward.

"No, that's fine," Hazel assured them. "This won't take long. And I have a dishwasher. But thank you anyway."

In truth, she was growing anxious for the evening to end and breathed a sigh of relief when the time came to retrieve everyone's coats. Throwing caution to the wind, she offered hugs all around, albeit in awkward fashion.

When she at last closed her door, she leaned against it and looked over to the disaster-struck kitchen.

Not everything had gone perfectly. Hazel thought the turkey had been a bit dry, evidenced by how much gravy everyone had poured onto their plates. But it had been a good evening none-theless.

I did it! she thought with a grin, still leaning against the door.

Cleaning up took a long time. But finally, seated at the immaculate table, Hazel opened her journal. As the dishwasher hummed and gurgled, she jotted down the evening's details. Under the "Fran" column, she wrote of her attempts to improve their relationship and shorten the distance between them. Some relationships could be so difficult to gauge, but she believed she was moving in a good direction with her sister. At least she was trying.

Hazel thought back to a certain part of the previous morning's sermon. The pastor had said that God often directed people to be involved in the answers to their own prayers.

"Don't be idle. Don't be a parked car. Move and God will guide you."

I'm certainly not being idle, she told herself. *I am moving. Pretty fast, I'd say. I went to that French restaurant. I went to that café. I'm a teller again. And now I've had Fran and the family over for dinner.*

Hazel felt pleased with the progress she'd made so far by stepping out of her comfort zone, yet she felt as though she was the one putting in the effort, doing all the work. Maybe these little changes had nothing to do with God answering her prayers. Maybe they were just the results of making her own choices to improve her life. What was God doing? Was he doing anything? She felt irreverent for thinking that way, but still she wondered.

ELEVEN

Calgary

THROUGHOUT OCTOBER, HAZEL kept an eye out for any lonely receipts that might cross her path. But none came by.

November brought bitter cold, snow, and strong winds to blow all that snow around. She seldom thought about receipts anymore. The likelihood of seeing one was already rare, but finding one in the midst of a snowbank seemed impossible.

On the third Sunday in November, Hazel felt disappointed that the pastor had come to his last sermon in the prayer series. She had found them enjoyable and challenging and didn't want to let go of this lifeline. She couldn't help but wonder whether anyone else in the congregation had begun keeping a prayer journal. Despite her attempts to mingle after each service, she never asked anyone.

Hazel stood around after the service with coffee in hand, patting herself on the back for making these little efforts. She had decided not to rush off to her empty apartment where nothing important needed to be done.

No one seemed to be in a hurry to leave the warm sanctuary and Hazel eventually found herself standing beside Margaret—

ninety-year-old Margaret, with a walking cane in one hand and a cookie in the other.

After an uncomfortable moment, Hazel broke the silence. "How are you doing today, Margaret?"

"I'm doing well. And you, Hazel? How are you doing?"

"I've been doing well too…" She trailed off. "I've really enjoyed the sermons on prayer."

"Oh yes, dear. Wonderful sermons."

"There's always so much to learn. It's kind of sad to have the series end."

"Yes. Come with me."

Margaret popped the last bit of cookie into her mouth and began walking down the hallway, unaware whether Hazel was following or not. Like an obedient dog, Hazel fell into step behind her, never having realized how fast a person using a cane could move.

When they reached the end of the hallway, Margaret stopped at a door marked with a piece of paper emblazoned with the words "Prayer Room." They entered the tiny, dimly lit space, which Hazel realized was no longer a prayer room since those prayers had been taken upstairs some time ago, as well as into the proverbial cloud.

Hazel followed Margaret up to two cluttered bookcases, representing the entirety of the church's small library. Few over the age of eighty seemed to even remember the church had a library, which might as well have been established before the invention of the paperback. Dull, cloth-covered books, each one looking like an ancient text, took up most of the shelf space. The books were crammed together so tightly that Hazel doubted she'd be able to slide a sheet of paper between them.

"I often come in here," Margaret said.

Hazel wondered why but said nothing. Next to the old woman, she felt a bit like a young student being mentored by a wise professor.

"There's a book here you might like. It's a little hard to see."

Hazel stepped up alongside her. "So what are we looking for?"

"Ah, here it is."

"Oh good," Hazel replied, perhaps too enthusiastic to leave this stuffy room behind.

Margaret handed Hazel a thin book. "Yes, I think you'll like this one."

Hazel could find no provision for checking out books, so she concluded that it must operate according to the honour system: take a book, then return it. And if she didn't return it, she doubted anyone would even notice—or care.

As they proceeded back up the hall, Margaret turned to Hazel, her face alight with concern.

"I need to find the Allens," she said. "I don't want them to leave without me."

"Oh, I'm sure they won't. We'll look for them back in the fellowship room."

Indeed, it only took a few moments to locate Mr. and Mrs. Allen, still holding full cups of coffee as they stood chatting with friends.

Hazel bundled herself up in her coat, scarf, toque, and mitts and left the church, tackling the half-block trek to her car with her head bent down. The temperature hovered around minus-thirty-two degrees Celsius and the wind added several degrees of further misery.

Near her car, Hazel noticed the corner of a small white piece of paper flapping in the wind. She bent down to retrieve it, needing to remove one of her bulky mittens. The beige crocheted scarf that crossed half her face hid her grin. This was undeniably a receipt!

She hurried around to the car door, her exposed hand maintaining a firm grip on the paper as her face stung from the cruel wind.

Inside, she immediately started up the car, wondering why remote starters had to be so astronomically expensive. It never seemed to be in her budget. With the engine running, she shivered and read over the receipt's details.

Changing her plans for the afternoon, she drove over to the university district, so close that it didn't allow enough time for the car's engine to warm up. Traffic remained light and finding a parking spot in the trendy neighbourhood proved no problem.

She entered a sparsely occupied bistro.

"Hi, I'd like a large caramel macchiato," Hazel said when she approached the counter.

The attendant looked up. "With whipped cream?"

"No thank you."

After finding a spot by the window, she took her first sip and gagged. *Well, this was a mistake. It's nothing but sugar! Who would drink this?*

Hazel pictured the person who'd bought this drink. She was probably a university student. Possibly a young girl, just out of high school. She might even be skinny, but she'd be chubby, as well as broke, if she kept ordering these things. What a waste of money.

On the subject of wasting money, Hazel thought about Maddie. They had become chattier at work. Most Monday mornings, Maddie talked about the nightclubs she'd visited or the clothes she'd bought. They were expensive-looking clothes, which Maddie tended to layer, showing off undulating hem lengths and colour combinations that Hazel would never entertain. There was nothing calm or symmetrical about them.

All those clothes must cost her a fortune. How can she possibly afford it all?

Since Hazel generated the paycheques, she knew how much Maddie made each month. It wasn't much above minimum wage. The poor girl must be living paycheque to paycheque.

Hazel wanted to help, but she had no idea how to manage it without being intrusive. She didn't want to preach about how one should spend money. Did Maddie save anything for the future? Did she invest? She probably didn't even have a TFSA. In fact, she probably didn't know the difference between a TFSA, GIC, or RRSP.

Hazel shook her head and wondered how this next generation of young adults would ever survive.

The macchiato grew cold—not that it mattered to Hazel. She managed to drink about a quarter of it, then drained the rest into a tiny sink near the receptacle for dirty dishes. She felt she'd be sick if she drank any more.

Looking for a positive from this latest adventure, she was happy to have discovered a new coffee place. She was also glad to have updated herself on the latest developments near the university. The district's progress in recent years amazed Hazel, with its tree-lined streets, shops, and greenspaces—well, whitespaces for now—and so many new condominiums built and ready to rent.

Driving home, she considered how far these receipt adventures might go. At least this latest one had just been for another coffee. How simple! But what would she do if she found a receipt for a hundred grocery items? Or for something terribly expensive?

She reminded herself that she was under no obligation to even pick a receipt up off the ground in the first place. And she certainly didn't have to follow through on these purchases, as if they held some power to dictate the course of her life. All she needed was some help getting out of her rut.

That afternoon, Hazel ran into Praveen in the apartment lobby.

"It's been quite a while, Praveen. Did you get out to Montreal?"

With undying enthusiasm, Praveen chatted about his recent trip to visit his brother and all the new restaurants they had visited in Montreal.

"Any more trips planned in the new year?" asked Hazel.

"Plans are in the works to visit family in India soon. In the meantime, I'm looking at going back to Europe, probably in January."

Hazel didn't think it possible, but the sparkle in his eyes seemed to brighten.

"Going back? How many times have you been over to Europe?"

"Well, let's see now… four? Yes, I think it's four. My plan is to stay in London a few days. Then take the train up to Scotland. I've always wanted to see Edinburgh. How fascinating it would be to walk along the ancient Royal Mile every day and explore the shops and cafes, and of course the castle and cathedral!"

"Isn't January rainy and cold—you know, that damp kind of cold? People always say a dry cold is easier to manage than a damp cold. But I wouldn't know."

"I find Britain rather chilly and rainy any time of the year. But Hazel, with all there is to see inside cathedrals, castles, museums, and art galleries, I can't say that I suffer!"

As they chatted, Hazel tried to envision herself in London. She could picture some of the more famous places, like Trafalgar Square, Tower Bridge, and the Tower of London. Then she imagined herself in an ancient European cathedral. On the British mystery shows she watched, people were constantly being murdered in historic churches. She quickly placed herself standing in one, amidst the rich ambiance of history, dark wood, stone, and silence.

They continued chatting for another fifteen minutes.

As she rode the elevator up, her mind continued to fixate on that picturesque imaginary church. Hazel believed that strolling around such a building would be the ultimate adventure. If she'd ever thought to make a bucket list, that would be right at the top.

Later that afternoon, Hazel opened the book Margaret had pulled off the shelf for her, a volume entitled *Answers to Prayer* by George Müller. She couldn't find the publication date on the first few yellowed pages and thumbed through the rest, scanning the tiny serifed print. The chapters were headed with Roman numerals.

The first chapter was called "Beginning and Early Days of the Orphan Work." As she read, she found it easy enough to comprehend, despite Müller's journals dating back to 1836. She smiled with amusement at his account of his ministry. It almost seemed at times like he was addressing her personally, referring to her as "dear esteemed reader."

I am a dear esteemed reader. How about that!

Before she knew it, an hour and a half had passed. Müller's lifestyle of prayer had dominated all that he did. Day by day, he'd wait for God's provision of his basic needs, as well as the needs of one hundred children and staff at his orphanage. What impressed Hazel was his careful accounting of the organization's funds and donations. He knew exactly how much had been donated to the orphans' cause at any given time, what costs would soon be incurred, and therefore how much to ask God for. He kept track of every pound, shilling, and penny, including the half-penny and the farthing.

Hazel designated the back pages of her prayer journal to Müller's prayer principles. That afternoon, she wrote out three.

- I brought even the most minute circumstances concerning the Orphan-House before the Lord in my petitions.
- His glory was my chief aim.
- It is a sufficient provision for the exigency of to-day... Tomorrow, as it brings its demands, will find its supply.[1]

At this rate, Hazel thought she'd most likely end up recording a quote from each of the book's ninety-four pages. It was all so good.

---

[1] George Müller, *Answers to Prayer* (Bolton, ON: A.E.C. Brooks, 2017), 14–15.

TWELVE

Paris

ON A MORNING in early December, a taxi left Brielle standing on a tree-lined street looking up at an unfamiliar apartment complex. Gentle snow had fallen on Paris's streets and the chilly wind had blown skiffs along the sidewalks. Brielle stood in the cold, trying to make up her mind.

Even knowing that Jean-Paul was out of town and would be gone for at least a week, she felt nervous. What explanation would she give if a neighbour asked about her presence? But then she didn't think Jean-Paul had much to do with his neighbours.

Still, she hesitated. The thought of spying on her son felt wrong.

She walked away and turned onto Rue Falguière, hoping to find a nearby café where she could sit, think, and decide whether to go through with her plan.

Instead she found a church, Saint-Jean-Baptiste-de-La-Salle.

Brielle knew about St. Jean-Baptiste-de-La-Salle and his good works back in the seventeenth century, but she didn't know much about the white brick building named after him, other than it had been built in the twentieth century. Cheery, light-coloured walls greeted her upon pulling open the wooden door. The sanctuary stood empty, and in the silence she walked over to a small plain table and lit a tea candle. She placed it back on the table and watched the flame for a moment.

She strolled up the aisle, halfway stopping to make the sign of the cross, and then took a chair. It wasn't a big building and the altar at the front was by no means ornate.

Feeling left in the dark about her son's life, Brielle tried to pray but couldn't offer up any specific information to God. So her words again revolved around wanting her son to be happy and led to a more suitable job.

As always, she had no idea how her prayers would be answered. Some days she believed God would bring about wonderful changes. Other days she wondered whether God even existed. But prayer always seemed to help.

Before leaving, she prayed one last time about going into Jean-Paul's apartment. She prayed that if she decided to enter, somehow she would be encouraged by what she saw.

By the time she exited the church, she had made up her mind. She headed straight to Jean-Paul's apartment building, telling herself that this escapade was based on the love and concern she had for him. She also knew Marie would hound her until she had investigated the apartment.

She opened the front door and began climbing the narrow curved staircase, pausing to catch her breath before stepping onto the third floor. She feared that a sudden change of plans would have Jean-Paul sitting in his apartment or arriving home any minute. She was risking their mother-son relationship and wondered whether this was worth it.

With a shaking hand, she inserted the apartment key. She opened the door, only to be confronted by a hollow, echoey entry. She had no doubt no one was home.

She stepped into the living room to see an uninviting white sofa with matching chair. Beside the sofa, a lone lamp stood askew. A stone-top coffee table that must have cost thousands of euros held nothing except the remote to the wall's flatscreen. The dominating feature of the room was its emptiness, from the floor all the way up to the vaulted ceiling. Only the Persian rug offered any sense of warmth; it looked out of place.

On the wall, Brielle recognized the three large-framed photographs of modern Paris that Jean-Paul had also hung in his former apartment, back when architecture had been so key in his life. These were the buildings of the city's financial district. She remembered him talking about them—their glass, steel, and granite all combining to create strong, modern, lines. He'd especially loved La Grande Arche.

Now Brielle stared at these same pictures, hung too far apart as if desperate to fill the cavernous space.

She proceeded on her slow walk into other rooms.

In the spartan, joyless dining and kitchen area, Brielle detected no smell. She felt relieved that she'd chosen not to wear her usual Chanel 19 perfume. She didn't want to leave a lingering scent. No wineglasses stood by the sink, as Marie had supposed. His fridge held only a few bottles of red wine, bottles of water, and some condiments. A few trays of ice cubes sat in the freezer. The trash bin held nothing.

She examined the other rooms. The bathroom countertop held a few toiletries and the towels were nicely hung, giving evidence of at least some life. The only vibrant feature of his bedroom, besides books, was the closet and its adequate assortment of fine clothes, both casual and formal, hanging on substantial wooden hangers.

Before leaving, Brielle stood at the balcony doors, looking out at Les Invalides. She told herself that she had done her best as a single mother, raising a boy whose father had abruptly left just after Jean-Paul's seventh birthday. Was there anything she could have done differently? He had always been quiet, keeping to himself, and only ever having a few friends throughout his school years.

Once again she reflected that he had seemed fine at his previous job. She'd even met a woman he once dated. Brielle had been hopeful that a serious relationship would develop, but it hadn't seemed to last long. "We're just not compatible," Jean-Paul had told her.

And now he'd become solitary and distant. He never talked about friends and he certainly never mentioned relationships with women.

Brielle didn't feel like she knew her son at all.

She was quick to turn her back on this depressing place. The visit had only left her with more questions. Truthfully, she wished she had never come.

* * *

Brielle glanced around at the alternating frescoes and paintings mounted on both sides of the nave at Saint-Louis d'Antin. In the latter part of the eighteenth century, King Louis XVI had commissioned its construction; in the nineteenth century, Pope Pius VII had visited on the occasion of Emperor Napoleon's coronation.

Part of her wanted to move up and get a better view of the outstanding artwork, but then she reminded herself why she had come. She disciplined herself to pray, even though it often brought her to tears. She could return another time to walk through the building and admire it like a museum.

Since entering Jean-Paul's lifeless apartment a week ago, her prayers had grown wordier. Feeling desperate, she asked God to allow something to happen in his life. Nothing bad, but something to steer him in a new direction.

The more she spoke, the more honest her prayer became. She told God not only about Jean-Paul and his needs, but also about herself, her worries and fears. She even acknowledged her own faith and how little it was. Approaching God in such an honest manner made her feel a touch of hope.

Brielle left the church and walked toward the Galleries Lafayette to meet up with Marie. On her way, she passed a *boulangerie* just as a customer was entering. The aroma of fresh baked bread was enticing, as was the window display of *baguettes* and *pain de campagne*. A short distance away, she eyed the window of a *pâtisserie* showing off straight rows of *éclairs*, *beignets*, *pain au chocolat* and an assortment of always delightful, not to mention colourful, *macarons*.

She also appreciated the signs of Christmas. Brielle wondered if the tourists found Paris's understated elegance a welcome relief from the gaudy holiday displays splashed across so much of the world.

She reached Angelina's with its white pillars, chandeliers, and dark wood, a favourite spot for lunch within the Galleries Lafayette. The chill of winter inspired her to order coffee before entrées. And as soon as their coffees were set down, Marie asked her inevitable question.

"So have you gone into his apartment yet? Any signs?"

Brielle felt annoyed but prepared for the interrogation. "Yes, last week I went there. He said he'd be away in Austria."

"*Bien*. And what did you discover?"

"There was nothing to discover, Marie. Everything looked clean and tidy, as I would have thought. He has lovely furniture. A white sofa and an exquisite stone-covered coffee table. Not much in his fridge, but I wouldn't expect there to be. He still has his books on architecture. Such wonderful books. And, as always, his closet is well-stocked and organized."

Brielle didn't mention her feelings of being overwhelmed, nor the apartment's sterility. The memory of her visit still produced pain in her heart.

"It was worth a try, don't you think?" Marie said. "But I can tell that you still worry, and I think you worry too much."

Brielle didn't consider the recent increase in her emotional turmoil as having been worth the try, although she admitted to Marie that she worried more than she should.

She went on to explain her new habit of entering churches to pray for her son.

Marie's eyebrows arched. "Really? And have you had any answers to these prayers of yours?"

"*Non.* Not as such. But I think I feel more at peace. I believe in God, Marie. I believe he wants to answer our prayers."

Marie hunched her shoulders. "Well, Brielle, you do whatever you want. But you only go into Catholic churches, *n'est-ce pas?*"

"*Mais oui.*" She didn't want Marie to know that she believed Protestant churches would be just fine. She just hadn't come across any yet.

Satisfied with Brielle's apartment news, and having no interest in further discussing churches or faith, Marie changed the topic.

"Now about my family. I have exciting news!"

Marie proudly announced the upcoming wedding of her granddaughter, to be held in April. A lively discussion of flowers, décor, and caterers occupied the next hour. Brielle was more than happy to talk about the wedding, of course, knowing the topic would surely dominate many of their future lunches.

THIRTEEN

Calgary

HAZEL'S CAR CREPT past several others lining the street before she found a place to park. She stepped out of her car into the winter stillness, where fresh snow muffled all sound, save for the crunch of her boots where neighbours had yet to shovel their sidewalks. There was no wind, no breeze, no movement of any air at all—nothing to disturb the magical winter tableau.

Before walking up to Fran's door, Hazel stood completely still and took in the grey skies, frosted trees, and omnipresent white. The scene overwhelmed and exhilarated her, forcing her to admit that winter, at times, held a powerful beauty, one with which the other seasons could not compare.

She also paused to appreciate the beauty of the warm white glow of perfectly symmetrical Christmas lights outlining Fran and Roger's house.

Both sisters embraced the Christmas season. Ever since Hazel could remember, their parents had made Christmas fun and festive. When their parents had died, they'd put in the effort to gather each December—a tradition that had gone on for decades. Hazel was glad for it, otherwise the sisters would never see each other.

Getting together at Christmas honoured their parents. But they only ever met at Fran's place, of course.

Hazel felt especially eager this Christmas. Since she'd already seen Fran twice recently, the usual awkwardness and anxiety had eased. She had to concede that not everything about her sister was awful. Fran had a heart for hospitality and often invited others over for Christmas dinner. She had the house, space, and money to do it lavishly.

Roger greeted Hazel warmly and took her coat as she stepped down from the landing, her feet sinking into the plush carpet. Roger introduced her to their new neighbours and an assortment of church members, some of whom she recognized from previous years. The atmosphere was festive, the conversations lively, and the music nostalgic. Somewhere in the background she heard the gentle refrains of "We Wish You a Merry Christmas." The scent of cranberries, probably from candles, joined the unmistakable whiffs of roast turkey.

Hazel eyed the three white Christmas trees, two of them reaching toward the vaulted ceiling in the living room; the one in the dining area was shorter but just as elegantly decorated in silver, gold, and white. Five massive white poinsettias were positioned around the room, drawing the eye from one to the next. The room was worthy of a home décor magazine.

Who else but Fran would feature three Christmas trees on the main floor? She doesn't have a minimalistic bone in her body, but they do look absolutely beautiful. They're perfect. Everything is so perfect.

She thought about her own modest tree, only waist-high and plopped in front of her balcony door. Its ornaments of many colours gave a joyful flair. Hazel had done her best to display the ornaments in some kind of pattern. Each ornament held a personal meaning or remembrance, and she felt obligated to keep each one. Last year, when Hazel and Julie had helped in Sunday school, one little girl in the class had crafted a snowflake ornament and presented it to Hazel. She'd felt so honoured to receive the hand-crafted ornament adorned with ribbons and glitter.

A snowflake like that—bursting with orange, lime green, and brown—would have upset the whole balance of Fran's immense living room. But the ornament looked fine on Hazel's tree, although she always placed it toward the back.

With a cup of hot cider in hand, Hazel drifted among the guests, listening to their chatter and enjoying the warmth of the fireplace. She was delighted to spot David, Aunt Peggy's son. It was good to see that Fran had kept in contact with him since the funeral.

It wasn't until Hazel headed into the kitchen that she encountered Fran standing at her massive granite island. She wore a cranberry-coloured sweater that complemented her complexion, along with a thick gold necklace and gold drop earrings. Hazel felt a stab of envy for wanting to look so good and regretted her choice to wear such a plain beige sweater.

Several other women scurried around the counters fulfilling their delegated tasks. At least everyone seemed to be enjoying their time; all Hazel saw were smiles, and all she heard was laughter.

Fran was making a fresh pot of coffee when she noticed her sister. Hazel wished Fran would put down the tin of coffee and come over to greet her with a hug and wish her a merry Christmas.

But that was not their relationship.

"Hi. Glad you made it," Fran said, extending Hazel a quick glance. "Help yourself to some... oh, I see you already got some cider. Good. Does anybody know where I put the coffee filter? I just had it in my hand."

It took a moment for Hazel to realize she wasn't talking to her any longer. Hazel turned back to the gathering and found a place to sit by one of the glittering white trees.

The interaction in the kitchen stayed with her, though—or rather, the lack of interaction. It saddened Hazel. She felt hurt and her heart was heavy while everyone else smiled and laughed. Shouldn't sisters have a special kind of relationship? Shouldn't it show strength and understanding, a result of experiencing life together under the same roof?

Ben came over and occupied a chair next to Hazel, drawing her into a conversation about how her work was going. Later, Hazel initiated a discussion with a couple nearby. She surprised herself at the ease with which she engaged in small talk. It was becoming easier for her to slip into, something she used to always leave to others.

The buffet-style turkey dinner was fabulous and Hazel didn't hold herself back from indulging in a second helping.

In previous years, Hazel hadn't stayed long after dinner. She would eat and then leave, at least when it was polite enough to do so. But this Christmas, as the crowd dwindled, Ben asked her to hang on for a bit.

When there remained only Hazel, Fran, Roger, David, and a few neighbours who seemed more like family, Ben broke some news.

"I have something to share with everyone. I'm getting married!" He paused, giving the assembled group a moment to react. "My fiancée, Megan isn't here, because she's spending Christmas day with her parents. But I can't wait for all of you to meet her. We are thinking of a couple of possible dates in May for the wedding. We'll let you know about the details as we get things sorted out."

Fran was quick to pipe in. "Roger and I already knew this, of course. We've met Megan, and what a lovely lady she is! We couldn't be happier. Now, I'll be hosting a spring bridal shower, and I'll get that information out to all you ladies soon."

Hazel felt delighted and longed to learn more about their relationship. Where had Ben and Megan met? Had it been love at first sight?

At nine o'clock that evening, Hazel left the bright lights of Fran's home and walked back to her car, accompanied only by the crunch of her boots in the stillness. She looked up to the cloud cover, now revealing a hazy full moon. Hazel marvelled at the sky, so beautiful that it reminded her of an impressionist's painting.

* * *

Hazel took only Christmas and Boxing Day off. She felt no need for a break and preferred to be in the office, occupied with meaningful work. The business had semi-thrived in November and early December, but now Evergreen was primed to function on a skeletal staff over the holidays.

After Boxing Day, Hazel arrived at work in proper business attire but anticipating little business. She often found herself alone at the front reception counter, working on her laptop and answering the rare call while Maddie took extra days off.

The days dragged and Hazel worked hard to keep occupied. She double-checked several account balances. She checked online for mistakes on their website and social media accounts, ensuring that every company name had its appropriate *Ltd.* or *Inc.*

She was bored.

On December 31, at 10:30 a.m., Mr. Lee walked around the building, visiting each employee who had come in to work and told them to go home at noon.

"After all, it's New Year's Eve!"

Most employees who had been there long enough knew that Mr. Lee always said this. And most had plans to leave work early anyway.

At noon, Hazel packed up her things. She took down her scenic wall calendar, which she would replace it with one she'd buy at half-price in mid-January. She tore off the last desk calendar quote as well, hearing Julie say, "You are never too old to set a new goal or to dream a new dream."[2] It was apparently a C.S. Lewis quote, and one that prompted Hazel to stop by Mr. Lee's office before leaving. She wanted to share with him an idea she had yet to act upon. Her new goal. Her little dream. A way to help others at work, especially Maddie.

Her idea had materialized in early November while sipping that nauseating macchiato.

---

[2] C.S. Lewis, *Goodreads*. "You are never too old…" Date of access: October 14, 2025 (https://www.goodreads.com/quotes/3189131-you-are-never-too-old-to-set-a-new-goal).

"I've been thinking of the other staff here—such as Maddie, Jordon, Erica, and a few others... I can't recall their names just now. But I wanted to offer them an opportunity to invest in a savings or retirement plan. That is, if they want to. Many other companies do this."

"That sounds interesting," Mr. Lee murmured.

"And I think it could be helpful. An agreed amount is automatically taken off each paycheque and deposited into a savings account at their bank. It doesn't have to be much. Even just thirty-five dollars a month accumulates, so that in three years they have painlessly tucked away more than twelve hundred dollars, plus interest."

Mr. Lee grinned at Hazel's enthusiasm. "That's a great idea, Hazel. Why don't you investigate how to implement it? And in the new year, check to see who wants to participate. Oh, and speaking of money, I've been looking at... well, I've been considering several things. I'm no longer allowing employees to choose vacation *pay*. Instead I want them to take vacation *time*. After all, that's what it's for. I'm counting the cost and looking at ways the company can save money. As you know, the business has seen better years. Most employees do take time off, but I don't think you've ever taken two weeks off at once."

Hazel, who much preferred to have the money rather than the time off, hesitated.

"No, I've never taken my full allotted time off," she finally admitted. "I really don't know who would handle the accounting for two whole weeks?"

"I'm sure we'd work something out. Maddie could keep an eye on things. I'd be around as well to make sure all is running smoothly. And my wife, Sophie... she's done some bookkeeping in her time. She's retired from the hair salon and could come in if needed. I suppose if you could avoid being away at the beginning and end of the month, that would be helpful. Hazel, as senior staff, you get first choice. Think about what two weeks you'd like to take off this year. And about that investment idea, we'll get things rolling. Good then. Happy new year, Hazel!"

"And you too, Mr. Lee."

That evening, with potato chips and mixed nuts on the coffee table, Hazel held a New Year's Eve party for one in front of the television. She tried to follow the shows highlighting the year in review, but instead she kept going back to the concerns she had carried all afternoon.

What on earth was she going to do for two weeks? She didn't need a vacation. She didn't *want* a vacation. And leaving her work in the hands of Maddie? Now that was terrifying.

How could Mr. Lee think so little of my position, as if anyone on the planet could do my job? she asked herself. *A person has to be good with numbers. And they need a sixth sense to know when something doesn't add up.*

Until now, Hazel had never felt undervalued at work. Now she wondered just how dispensable she could be at Evergreen Printing.

Eventually, she returned her attention to the television and began considering her own personal year in review. Progress had been made. She felt good about the little adventures she'd embarked on. She was getting out and about again and even getting more involved at church, helping to count the offering money and staying after the service to chat. And in wanting to live with a greater sense of purpose, she had come up with her savings plan for the employees at work. She wasn't sure, but perhaps the situation with Fran had even improved an iota.

It had been months since the start of her prayer journey, and Hazel still wondered where God was in all this. So many of her improvements were due to her own decisions to make changes. Did any of this have to do with God? She wished she felt his presence. Was he specifically directing her or was she just making good choices of her own doing?

Maybe it's a combination, she considered. *God's directing me as I make choices. Surely he must be doing something to answer my prayers, but I just don't see it. And now with having to take vacation time this year… well, is this part of God's plan? What on earth am I going to do with my two weeks off?*

She recalled her pastor talking about the unseen presence of God in a previous sermon. He'd expounded on a verse in Psalms, applying it to the exodus story of God guiding the Israelites through the Red Sea.

Hazel got up from her couch and returned with her Bible. When she finally found the passage, Psalm 77:19, she read it out loud.

"Your path led through the sea, your way through the mighty waters, though your footprints were not seen."

Prayer is all about faith in God. I can't see God. I can't see his footprints. I can't detect his movements. And I know my prayer requests are good requests.

There was nothing wrong with asking for adventure, or ways to help people, or to be closer to Fran. And God wanted to give good things to his children. She just needed to keep going forward, walking with God, believing that he heard her and was the one guiding her.

Hazel came back to the television in time to hear the lively maritime music from a gathering in Newfoundland. She also saw people in Iqaluit standing out in the snow, dancing near an outdoor stage where musicians entertained in the cold. She watched crowds gather for the countdown in Vancouver, a weather hotspot where the temperature hovered above freezing. Soon she heard shouts as the various crowds counted backwards from ten.

Hazel raised her glass of ginger ale and said, rather flatly, "Happy new year, Hazel."

FOURTEEN

Calgary

IN EARLY JANUARY, Arctic air had penetrated every surface in the city: brick, asphalt, sandstone, and soil. The nighttime temperatures hovered around minus-thirty-five degrees Celsius and peaked at minus-twenty-five on a good day. With only eight hours of daylight, Hazel went to work in the dark, returned home in the dark, and in between, when daylight existed, sat in her windowless office.

One such day, Hazel approached Maddie with her tax-free savings account idea. At the sound of the word *invest*, Hazel detected a shot of alarm on Maddie's face. As they chatted, Hazel correctly assumed that Maddie knew nothing about the advantages of a TFSA. They even went out for lunch to discuss setting things up.

But the investment idea ended there.

"Thanks, that sounds great," Maddie said as they walked back to the office. "I know it's important to save money. And at least this job is making me put money into my Canadian pension thingy, so I'll have some money to retire on. Anyway, I'll give it some thought."

Hazel wanted to tell the young woman that her "Canadian pension thingy" wouldn't provide anywhere near enough money to retire on. But they'd already discussed a lot of financial scenarios and she didn't want to push her agenda too hard.

Over the coming month, Maddie never did give Hazel the go-ahead to proceed. Even when Maddie received her January paycheque, she never said anything to Hazel about investing a portion of it.

Her discussions went similarly with Jordon and Erica, except Hazel didn't bother taking them out for lunch.

She didn't let the lack of interest bother her. She knew she had done a good thing. She had tried to be helpful and would continue to be available should a ray of interest ever shine.

· · ·

By the end of January, southern Alberta had experienced a few chinooks, but only minor ones with the winds bringing slightly warmer temperatures for a day. In mid-February, the chinook winds once again arrived from the west. Having dispensed their moisture over the Rockies, they swooped down over the southern part of the province with their dry, warm air.

The temperature in Calgary shot up to eleven degrees from minus-eighteen. Snow and ice melted into slush, turning every vehicle an ugly grey. The combination of frequent vehicles and large puddles proved unfortunate for many a pedestrian.

Despite these little upsets, most people appreciated the reprieve from the cold.

Hazel took an afternoon off work to attend a dental appointment. Walking toward the building, she felt the warmth on her face. She imagined herself sitting out on her balcony at home, enjoying a coffee—just because she could. It was a small act, but nonetheless a luxury in February without risk of frostbite and hypothermia.

She walked past waist-high mounds of snow, freshly cleared and piled by the plough. The snow was already dimpled by the warmth of the sun and wind.

Then she saw it: a receipt sticking out from the remains of a snowbank. She felt surprise, since she hadn't thought about receipts for a long time. The top of the small piece of paper fluttered in the wind, almost as if it were waving to her, wanting to be rescued.

She retrieved it and read its details.

A sports bag! Well, at least it wasn't another coffee.

She pocketed the receipt and glanced back at the big box store behind her, the same store where this stranger had recently made the purchase.

As the hygienist scraped and polished Hazel's teeth, all Hazel could think about was what she would do with a sports bag. She had no use for one. What would she put in it?

There must be someone I could give it to, she thought. *But who? Too bad it wouldn't make a decent bridal shower gift.*

Her thoughts turned to the stranger who'd bought the original bag. She imagined a mom buying it as a birthday present for her son or daughter. Then, out in the parking lot, while reaching for her car keys, the wind had whipped the receipt away.

After the appointment, Hazel walked to the store, unzipped her coat, and avoided a puddle of slush. She looked for a similar bag and found one that was the exact same price. The details on the receipt provided no information about the original bag's colour, so she had to make a choice.

Hazel soon stood in line at the checkout holding the red sports bag. As she neared the cashier, she overheard the girl ask the customer in front of her, "Would you like your receipt?"

The customer's snarky response surprised Hazel.

"Why would I want a silly receipt?"

Hazel sighed.

Someone should do a documentary on receipts, she mused. *There's something about the psychology of why some people love them, while others react as if they're worthless trash. It could explain when receipts were invented, how they've evolved over the years, and how they're slowly becoming extinct. Now that would be interesting.*

Hazel approached the cashier and smiled to demonstrate that she wasn't a bite-your-head-off kind of customer.

"This is a really nice bag!" the cashier exclaimed.

"Yes, it is."

Hazel hoped the cashier would say no more. She didn't want to wait around for her to ask something like, "Is it for the gym?" Hazel didn't want to lie ("Yes, it is. I go to the gym so often and need to replace my old drab one"). And she didn't want to tell the truth ("I have absolutely no idea what I'm going to do with this").

Fortunately, the cashier said nothing further.

At the end of the transaction, still feeling the need to compensate for the rudeness of the previous customer, Hazel smiled.

"Yes, I would love to have a receipt," she added. "I find they help me keep track of things. Thank you so very much!"

As she drove home, she had an idea as brilliant as the bag itself: she could donate the bag to the youth silent auction at church!

I hope they're having one this spring. They must be. They always do.

The following Sunday, after the service, Hazel scanned the congregation for any sign of Gloria.

"Gloria, do you know if the youth will be having a silent auction this spring?" she asked when she spotted her friend.

Gloria's face lit up. "We sure are! The auction, along with the chili dinner, will be held in the middle of March this year. Are you interested in helping?"

"No... it's not that. But I have an auction item I'd like to contribute."

Gloria's enthusiasm seemed to drop a little, but she maintained her smile. "Well, that will be great, Hazel!"

Hazel left church wondering why she had turned down helping with the auction and dinner. Saying *no* felt almost like an automatic response. She had helped with the auction many times before, but that had always been with Julie at the helm.

● ● ●

The uneventful winter weeks of January and February passed. Then, on a late Saturday afternoon in mid-March, Hazel found herself shredding blocks of cheddar cheese. She had been at the church since eleven that morning with the rest of the volunteers, preparing dinner for about eighty people. Chatter and laughter had filled the kitchen all day, along with the rich aroma of chili. Everyone had been sharing funny, interesting, and thoughtful stories from their own lives and the work they accomplished didn't seem like work at all.

At one point, Hazel smiled at someone's comment and looked up from opening another package of cheese. All the other volunteers were busying themselves with the preparations, and in that moment she felt joyful—and realized how much she had missed this sense of community. Hazel knew she was coming back around to enjoying life as she once had before her friend died.

She silently thanked God, sensing that her prayers were being answered. God must somehow be leading her. Perhaps he was doing something in her heart, giving the desire to make better choices. As she became aware of the opportunities around her, she'd started to say yes. And the continual lightness she felt in her spirit? Well, how could that be explained other than to conclude that God was working in her?

Later at the dinner, Hazel sat at a table with some of the volunteers she had worked alongside all afternoon. And once the plates were cleared away, she watched as the dinner guests walked around the side of the room, eyeing all the auction items and making bids.

Over and over, she checked back on the bidding war for the red sports bag. To her delight, it finally sold for close to twice the amount she had paid for it.

Hazel didn't stay long afterwards to help with the cleanup— not many of the older people did. The entire day had been busy and fun, but she felt undeniably exhausted. The youth had energy to burn this late in the day; Hazel didn't.

When she returned home, she met Praveen in the lobby. She hadn't seen him since the last week of January, when they'd talked all about his recent trip to Great Britain. They'd talked for a half-hour that day about exploring Edinburgh. Praveen had booked a hotel room near the Royal Mile and spent the entire trip walking everywhere.

"I forgot to check my mailbox today," he said, running a hand through his hair.

She noticed how tired he looked tonight and decided not to mention that it was Saturday, and of course mail wasn't delivered on Saturdays. She worried that his memory might not be what it once was.

They chatted only briefly, sensing each other's need for sleep.

Hazel mustered up the energy to update her journal that night. She'd had such a good time with her church friends and wrote a paragraph on the joy she felt over helping out a good cause. She couldn't remember laughing so much in a long time.

Before going to bed, she opened her bedroom window a crack and let the cool air drift in. Cool, but not cold. Spring was on its way. In fact, it would officially arrive in six days.

Thinking about spring and warmer weather, Hazel lay in bed, contemplating her vacation. She hadn't decided where to go yet, if anywhere, but she had at least chosen the timing: the middle two weeks of July.

"One of those weeks will line up with the Calgary Stampede," she had explained to Mr. Lee. "Since business everywhere is slow then, I thought it would be a good time to be away."

Mr. Lee had taken note of the dates and approved the vacation request.

Hazel had almost fallen asleep when she heard an unexpected patter against her windowpane. She sat up, listening intently, then bounded out of bed like a six-year-old on Christmas morning. She hurried to her bedroom window and slid it fully open. Drops of rain were visible under streetlights.

Hazel had never liked the rain. Sure, it watered the earth and caused plants to grow, but it also ruined perfectly laid plans. No one liked to get caught in the rain, getting wet, chilled, and miserable. Not much fun in that.

But this rain was different, and Hazel smiled. It signified the changing of the seasons and she couldn't help but celebrate the simple fact that it wasn't snow.

RAIN

He says… to the rain shower, "Be a mighty downpour."
—Job 37:6

FIFTEEN

Paris

MARIE'S GRANDDAUGHTER'S WEDDING took place in April at Église de la Sainte-Trinité. The church's sixty-five-metre belfry reached into the grey skies that threatened to pour down over Paris.

Brielle left the taxi and hurried into the church before the rain could fall in earnest. In the entryway, she paused to admire the ornate décor, appreciating this structure that was known to have been part of Baron Haussmann's beautification project of Paris back in the nineteenth century. There was much for the eye to take in, with the high altar, gallery organ, and enormous paintings, along with sculptures and side chapels with stained-glass windows.

While being escorted down the aisle, Brielle smiled as she passed bouquets of white roses, tied with French brocade vintage ribbon, just like she and Marie had talked about. She took a second look at the Trudon candles arranged on the table at the front, knowing those seven candles alone would have set Marie back almost six thousand euros.

It was a splendid service, and no one had expected anything less.

After the wedding, once most of the guests had gone, a few people mingled near the entryway. Instead of immediately returning home to rest for the afternoon, Brielle walked up the aisle, approaching the altar to perform her prayer ritual. She brought before God matters that surprised her for being unrelated to Jean-Paul; over the months, she had begun to feel a deeper personal connection with God.

The wedding's decadent ambience had her feeling happy, so she also thanked God for her friends and her life. She then concentrated on Jean-Paul and kept up her request for changes in his life. She even prayed that he would be drawn back into the architecture world.

After a few hours of rest, Brielle ventured out once again for the wedding reception. Holding an open umbrella over her head, she waited for a taxi to take her to Hall of the Men-at-Arms at La Conciergerie. She entered the ancient and cavernous hall as an attendant stepped forward to take her raincoat and dripping umbrella.

Brielle adjusted her lotus silk shawl, which wrapped around her full-length burgundy dress. Upon seeing the candles, flowers, hanging lights, and massive bouquets of golden balloons, her eyes brightened as though to echo the other amazed guests: *Oh, c'est magnifique. Très, très magnifique!*

After mingling for a time, the guests found their way to their designated tables. Brielle followed her usher to a table occupied by mostly familiar faces, although she had soon greeted and introduced herself to those she didn't know.

Once seated, Brielle began to feel uncomfortable, even a touch dizzy. She forced herself to engage in conversation.

But past memories of the Conciergerie surfaced, despite her efforts to keep them buried.

Almost seven decades ago, Brielle had huddled with her fellow nine-year-old classmates as they listened to their instructor, Monsieur Thibault. They had just walked the same ancient hallways, the same ones Marie Antoinette had walked destined for the guillotine. The class then entered this same stone-walled space, although at the time it had seemed massive, dim, and eerie. They'd gathered at the foot of a pillar where Monsieur Thibault pointed up to the words *Inondation 28 Janvier 1910*. A dark line on the pillar indicated how high the floodwaters had risen that day. The rain had been coming down hard as a terrified Brielle returned home, worried about floodwaters engulfing the city of Paris. Upon entering their apartment, Brielle's mother had informed her that her father had died in a car accident that afternoon. The rain had been a prominent factor in the three-car collision.

From then on, Brielle had always despised the rain. Mostly, she feared it.

Today Brielle avoided focusing on the writing on the pillar, so clear in her line of sight. She instead gazed across to the enormous vases of flowers and linen-draped tables aglow in candlelight. The tables showcased the best of Parisian hors d'oeuvres. She placed her attention upon the lovely place settings of cutlery and lace-patterned plates.

Over the course of the evening, Brielle tried to enjoy the food. She listened to the speeches and participated in brief interactions with Marie, but she couldn't help but remain uneasy.

When the reception wound down, Brielle hurried out. Back out in the rain, she stepped into the taxi and felt relieved that the evening had finally ended.

Sleep didn't come easily. Ensconced in her luxury apartment, she watched out her window as flashes of lightning lit up the rainy sky to the accompaniment of booming thunder. She grew increasingly worried about Jean-Paul and wondered how he was managing in Belgium.

She longed to be in a church, where she could light a tea candle, sit in a chair amongst a hundred empty ones, and pray. With each church visit, she had grown more dependent upon the ambience to help quiet her soul.

But now she got up, lit her own candle, and sat at her kitchen table. For the second time that day, she prayed for Jean-Paul's safety and happiness. Since being in the Conciergerie, she felt a growing urgency that he needed to leave his current job. She asked again for God to allow something to happen. Something that might make Jean-Paul quit his job. Maybe retire.

She spoke more words to God than she had ever spoken before to him, pressured by the bad feeling that haunted her. She opened her heart and shared her growing struggles, worry, and stress. She even mentioned her disappointment over Jean-Paul not following through to take her to the Festival Resonance at La Sainte Chapelle. Perhaps next year. The festival wasn't a huge concern, but it felt good to unburden herself before God.

• • •

Jean-Paul walked the cobbled streets of Bruges, appreciating each medieval building he passed. Once he reached Burg Square, in the city's centre, he sat on a bench waiting for his contact. He far preferred to communicate by text, but his Belgian contact had wanted to meet in person.

When the contact did arrive, he sat beside Jean-Paul. He didn't seem to be older than thirty and had a friendly manner. The two men easily slipped into an amicable conversation about rifles, revolvers, and international travel. As rain fell, both men threw aside the unwritten protocols they knew to follow and decided to step into a nearby pub.

The longer they talked, though, the more Jean-Paul became aware of the other man's incompetence. He sipped his wine slowly while his contact gulped down beer. Jean-Paul's list of adjectives grew the longer he watched and listened; this man was negligent, sloppy, and undisciplined.

Regretting his flippant decision to enter the pub, Jean-Paul tried to end the exchange. He then paid the tab for both men and left. The rain slowed down as he made his way back to the hotel and Jean-Paul appreciated the fresh air.

He paused on a bridge spanning a canal and looked down at the water, his thoughts turning to his father. He'd never known much about the man, other than that he'd been involved in real estate. One time when his father had been away for several days, Jean-Paul remembered asking his mother, "Why can't he just sell apartments in Paris? Why does he have to go all over France?"

His mother's reply hadn't provided any comfort. "Good questions, Jean-Paul."

But the childhood memory Jean-Paul recalled most clearly had happened when he was seven years old. His father had stopped what he was doing long enough to notice Jean-Paul sitting at the kitchen table, drawing a building. He commented on how good it was.

"Excellence will get you far in life," his father said. "When you find something you're good at, like drawing, go after it with all you've got. That will be your way forward."

Those complimentary and instructive words still held such weight. They were also the last words his father had ever spoken to him, because he had left them the very next week. It turned out that he had another woman, another home, another life in Toulouse that he much preferred.

Throughout his education, Jean-Paul had striven for excellence in everything he did. Since he loved to draw, it was no surprise that he pivoted toward architecture, an area in which he could indeed excel. And his work over the years had been highly valued and respected.

But as with most things in life, changes come. Eventually the company harped on budget cuts and demanded that he upsell to clients. He was supposed to inspire them to want something bigger, better. Jean-Paul and his colleagues had called this approach the Triple C's: cut corners creatively. And so the last three years of his career as an architect had been gruelling. Seldom did projects come in on budget, and never under budget. Squabbles with unhappy clients and managers became an almost daily occurrence.

He'd also struggled to tolerate the new generation rising to join the workforce. Whenever he met someone younger than himself, he watched for signs of excellence. Few ever showed any inclination to pursue it.

That had been true in the world of architecture and it was true now, in Bruges. Jean-Paul questioned the entire organization he'd joined and wondered how they could have sent him someone so incompetent.

He proceeded toward his hotel, growing frustrated at how long it took for him to find the correct street. How easy it was for him to give in to frustration these days. He so often deflected, recognizing the lack of excellence in others rather than noticing it in himself.

Back in his hotel room, he again considered the possibility of taking an early retirement. Why stay in this for another five years? Two years sounded so much better.

SIXTEEN

Calgary

ONE SATURDAY MORNING, Hazel stood on her balcony, remaining under the alcove to keep dry from the April showers. The heavy rains were greatly disappointing, as she had hoped to go for a long walk. She'd hoped the forecast might be wrong, as it often was, but not today.

Before going back inside, she heard voices below and the slam of a vehicle door. She stepped out into the rain to peer over the railing. An ambulance had taken command of the driveway. Two paramedics were rolling a stretcher into the building.

Since the ambulance hadn't arrived with blaring sirens, Hazel thought it must not be an urgent situation. Not a real emergency.

Then it occurred to her: someone may have died.

Regardless, she decided it would be a good time to take out her recycle bin, even though it contained only one flattened cracker box.

When the elevator doors opened to the main lobby, she heard voices from around the corner—from the same hallway as Praveen's apartment. Light shone from his open doorway and the paramedics could be heard speaking just inside.

Her heart raced as she hung back by the elevators, desperate for information but not wanting to appear nosy. She certainly didn't want to get in the way.

Finally, after ten minutes, she disposed of her cracker box and returned to her apartment. She wore her black raincoat and stood on the balcony like a sentry, the floppy hood obscuring her eyes. One could have mistaken her for an oversized plastic owl, were it not for her frequent movements. It wasn't long before she saw the paramedics carry the stretcher into the ambulance.

Praveen lay on the stretcher, an oxygen mask positioned over his nose and mouth. Hazel breathed in relief that he was still alive.

She had no real connection with Praveen apart from their mailbox interactions. She certainly had no way of getting in touch with his family. How would she find out if he was okay? She tried not to worry and then remembered the words of George Müller—not word for word, but the main concept. Her situation wasn't the same as his, although the same principle applied. Müller always gave his overwhelming feelings to God, seeking encouragement rather than worry. When the world expected him to be in great despair, he instead leaned on God's peace and omnipotence.

Knowing that God was her ultimate connection to Praveen, she prayed for his health and quick return. She thought of the sadness she'd feel if he died. Oh how she would miss him.

. . .

Two weeks later, upon arriving home from work, Hazel peered down the hallway towards Praveen's suite, as had been her habit of late. She'd even knocked on his door several times, to no avail. But this time she heard voices inside.

She knocked.

A woman pulled the door open, and behind her was another woman with her arms full of folded clothes.

"Hi, I'm Hazel," she said. "From the third floor. I haven't seen Praveen for some time but saw him taken away by ambulance. Is he all right?"

The scene before her confirmed that all was not right. Praveen's apartment was in a state of chaos as the women placed his belongings into boxes.

"I'm Rana and this is my sister Azita," said the woman who'd answered the door. "We're his daughters. Sorry to tell you this, but our dad died the same day he was taken to hospital. It was a heart attack."

Hazel could tell that Rana was working to maintain her composure.

"We were about to take a coffee break," Rana added, hesitating. "Would you like to join us?"

The three women sat around the cluttered kitchen table amidst the disorganization of boxes and items yet to find their way into one. Hazel had never been in Praveen's apartment before and she took the opportunity to glance at his clothes, books, and many framed family photos. The couch held stacks of books and files. It felt overwhelming.

"We'd run into each other down by the mailboxes and often chat for half an hour," Hazel murmured, expressing her condolences. "He was always so encouraging. I'm really going to miss our lobby moments. We both loved getting mail. Even flyers. I guess we both had an affinity toward paper."

"He loved paper too much," Azita agreed, sweeping her hand across the living room. "As you can see, our dad kept everything. Absolutely everything."

"Sorting through all his things has become like a travelogue," Rana added. "Brochures, papers, magazines from places he visited... he often visited our uncle in Montreal. And he travelled Europe several times. Britain had become one of his favourite places."

Hazel nodded. "Yes, we chatted about his time there in January. Sounded like he had a fantastic time galivanting all about. I always loved to hear about his adventures."

Rana turned to her sister. "There's so much to recycle here. I mean, look at that pile over there. I think I'll take some of that home to put in my own recycle bin. We're literally filling up the bins here. They'll be overflowing soon."

Hazel surveyed the piles of travel brochures and magazines and hoped the daughters weren't about to discard everything. Shouldn't some of them be organized, filed, and labelled for easy access later? But that was out of Hazel's control.

The subject shifted from the clutter of paper to the funeral, which had already been held the previous week. Hazel wished she had known it. Praveen's four brothers had flown in to attend. She felt great sadness over not having known more about Praveen's life or getting to meet his family.

Hazel finished her coffee and rose, leaving the daughters to carry on. She thanked them for their hospitality and again expressed her condolences.

• • •

Later that week, once again in the recycling room, Hazel saw the bins almost overflowing. Knowing it to be the work of Praveen's daughters, she couldn't help but smile. She thought about the wonderful old neighbour she had loved to chat with for seven years. No longer would he be part of her life.

Hazel added her small portion to the bins, thankful that they would be emptied the next day. She turned to leave, but then stopped when she noticed a slip of white paper on the floor. By its size and shape, she felt certain it was a receipt. She picked it up, read the details, then robotically made her way toward the elevators.

For the balance of the afternoon, Hazel either stood at her balcony window or sat on her couch. Wherever she stood or sat, she stared off into space. She reviewed the previous four receipts and how easy it had been to copy them. Venturing to those shops had been fun, getting her out of the house to try new places and have new experiences. She credited the sports bag receipt for having gotten her involved with the youth auction.

As she held this fifth receipt, though, she realized it must have belonged to Praveen. The date and place both corresponded with his travels. The receipt itself lent Hazel a connection with her former friend. But it also presented problems—preposterous and costly problems. The receipt was like an invitation. A vacation destination. A true adventure.

This is so much bigger than buying a coffee, she thought.

Was God guiding her with this little piece of paper? She wished she could answer a definitive yes or no.

She recounted a particular sermon about prayer, remembering that there were often three steps in dealing with a challenging situation. First, one had to pray, giving the situation to God and asking for direction. Second, depending on the situation, one had to arrive at a decision and act on it. Third, one had to trust God as they moved forward.

Pray. Choose. Trust.

She held the receipt, considering its implications. Her vacation time was coming up in three months. Should she remain home for two weeks, reading books and walking around the neighbourhood. Or should she fly to Edinburgh to buy a tartan umbrella?

SEVENTEEN

Calgary

AS THE RAINY month of April continued, Hazel made it a habit to hold open her black umbrella as she exited the bus and walked to work, all the while remembering Praveen's umbrella purchase in Edinburgh. His receipt was always top of mind, hanging over like a giant question mark.

The cool, damp weather soon slipped away, giving way to sunny skies in the first week of May. Hazel took advantage of the improvement by taking walks through the nearby park.

Those walks became prayer walks. On May 5, a day with particularly delightful weather, her walk was extensive. It was the one-year anniversary of Julie's death and Hazel had much to pray about. She poured out thanks to God for having gotten to know such a dear friend, and for knowing that she would see Julie again because of their mutual faith in Christ. She thanked God for her more active life; although she couldn't detect any exact movement of his hand, she chose to believe that he heard her prayers and was answering them in his own time and way.

At last she thanked God for the sun and warmth. She also prayed about her relationship with Fran, whom Hazel anticipated connecting with at Ben's upcoming wedding. God could use the process of sending out wedding-related texts and emails as a way of drawing them closer. She had come to expect that God would do wonderful things.

. . .

The long-range forecast for the day of Megan's bridal shower called for nothing but sunshine. But as mid-May drew closer, a mix of sun and cloud seemed favourable—and even, possibly, rain.

Nearing the day, Hazel phoned Fran to see whether she could do anything to help, knowing full well that her sister would rebuff her. If anything, Fran would find the offer annoying. Just the same, she hoped her gesture might at least be appreciated.

As expected, though, Fran insisted that she had everything under control. That said, her tone of voice had an unexpected touch of warmth and she went on to convey her plans for an extravagant outdoor gathering. Roger was to pick up four round tables from the church, then drive across the city to get chairs and sun umbrellas. Hazel listened as Fran read over the menu, overflowing with charcuterie boards and fruit piled high on platters. As soon as Fran mentioned the chocolate fountain, Hazel interjected to ask about whether she had a rainy-day plan.

"Well, of course I've considered that, Hazel," Fran snapped. "Why wouldn't I have? You'd think I've never arranged a thing in my life. I know very well that the forecast calls for a chance of rain. But I also know things can change, having lived here my *entire life.*" After letting out her pent-up stress, Fran took a deep breath and continued with less frustration. "Anyway, we'll manage just fine. And if we must bring everything indoors, we will. It will all work out."

When the day of the bridal shower arrived, Hazel found herself driving over to Fran's place through pouring rain, alternating the window wipers between intermediate speed and the fastest setting possible. She pulled up in front of Fran's house and took in the rivers of water flowing down the road in search of storm sewers. Solid grey clouds were locking in overhead and wouldn't clear until at least early evening.

Rain, rain, go away. But then I suppose showers for a bridal shower are appropriate.

She waited in the car, not wanting to arrive early in case Fran thought she had come to help. Ten minutes before the shower was to start, she approached the door, and walked in without bothering to ring the bell.

Inside she shed her raincoat and placed her umbrella in a corner next to a few others. She didn't see Fran, but several other guests were sitting and chatting. She noticed a young woman in the chair of honour, above which were perched balloons and ribbons.

The bride-to-be rose from the decorated chair and introduced herself to Hazel, who was impressed by the young woman's friendly and easy manner.

After chatting a bit, Hazel left in search of Fran. She found her sister standing by the kitchen sink, taking several painkillers. Her face lacked that radiant glow her expensive age-defying face products usually provided.

"Anything I can do to help?" Hazel bravely asked.

"Oh. Hi Hazel. Nope, everything's done. I'll be right out."

Taking that as a cue to exit, Hazel turned to leave. Before returning to the living room, though, she glanced back at Fran's turned back. Fran was staring out the window above the sink at the pelting rain.

On her way back to the party, Hazel passed the French doors that led to the backyard. Heavy rain was bouncing off the white tables, falling on the perfectly trimmed potentilla shrubs, soon to be bursting with yellow flowers. The red-potted geraniums were drenched, ready to be lifted into the garage at the threat of hail.

Hazel knew how much Fran liked to follow through with a plan, especially Plan A. Plan B was always inferior.

That's what's giving her a headache, Hazel decided. *She probably had everything set up only to have the rain ruin her plans. Then she had to drag everything back inside.*

Hazel remembered once hearing that the best plan wasn't Plan A or Plan B, but Plan G—God's plan. But she wasn't about to mention this to Fran, who likely wasn't open to hearing a sermonette at the moment.

She felt a surprising stab of empathy. She knew how hard Fran had worked to organize this, and how disappointed she must feel.

A stout woman in an uncomfortably tight-looking black pantsuit almost bumped into Hazel. Ignoring Hazel, the woman continued straight into the kitchen without so much as an apology for the near-collision.

"The coffee is ready, isn't it?" the stout woman asked Fran.

"Not yet," Fran replied. "But there's lots of punch."

Hazel knew the discipline it took for her sister to keep her voice light under these circumstances. She caught the stout woman's disapproving look.

Once they were alone, Hazel returned to Fran's side. "Who was that?"

"Ben's future mother-in-law. Can you believe it?"

Hazel offered a genuinely sympathetic look. "You know, maybe she's just really stressed, being the mother of the bride and all that."

"Doesn't matter. She doesn't have to be such a cow."

"Maybe we just need to get to know her better?"

"Yeah, maybe. Anyway, Hazel, we'll get through this. I'll be out in a minute."

Hazel returned to the living room, feeling a touch of warmth from their brief conversation.

We'll get through this. We, plural, as if I'm part of Fran's life. I'm part of this trying day!

As more people arrived and the afternoon progressed, the atmosphere settled down. Hazel enjoyed getting to know Megan and most of her family. She couldn't help but glance now and again out the windows and their view of the landscaped backyard and heavily treed valley in the distance. The rain continued to intensify the already vibrant green foliage.

When the bridal shower wound down and people began leaving, Fran didn't object to Hazel's offer to stay behind and clean up. As they carried dishes and platters from the living room to the kitchen, they didn't talk much. Even then, though, Hazel felt an unfamiliar degree of camaraderie with Fran.

Hazel left Fran's place feeling genuine sadness for her sister, considering her failed backyard plans and the bossy woman, bossier than Fran herself, soon to be related to her by marriage.

I know God is working in me, Hazel thought on the drive home. *Fran may not be changing, but I am. Maybe I'm understanding her more? I know she's stressed. She's disappointed. She's trying hard to do her best for Ben and Megan.*

But Hazel didn't like the way her mind had begun thinking in terms of the sisters sharing a common enemy—Megan's mother. It just wasn't right. It would have been better for the sisters to see the woman as a common challenge—the challenge being to get to know her better and understand what made her so blustery and rude.

. . .

On May 28, the morning of the wedding, Hazel enjoyed coffee and prayed on her balcony under a brilliant sun.

"Perhaps Fran and I can grow closer at tonight's reception, God," she said. "I know she's so stressed. Yes, she's organized a million things before, but never something as important to her as her son's wedding. Amidst all the busyness tonight, I pray that we'll have the opportunity to chat—to chat like so many other sisters do. And maybe, Lord, there can be some ice broken with Megan's mother. I know Fran is really struggling with her."

Hazel knew God didn't need ideas on how to improve people's relationships. Since before the beginning of time, God had always had plans to bring about his purposes. So although she expected the wedding and reception to unfold smoothly, she hoped and believed God could use that lovely setting to bring closeness and healing.

The ceremony was to take place at Fran and Roger's church. Hazel had been there a few times but still felt awestruck by this building, which had so many features Hazel's church didn't. A large lounge held six leather couches, coffee tables, and side tables. A cappuccino bar stood off to the side. The focal point belonged to the grand fireplace, magnificent even without a cozy fire burning.

An usher led Hazel down the aisle; tule fabric clasped the bouquets of baby's breath attached to the end of each pew. She sat in the third pew from the front, eying the other bouquets of pink and white roses.

The church soon filled and the service began. Hazel appreciated the predictability of the ceremony. At the start, both Fran and Megan's mother lit the front candles. They performed their tasks in rigid unison, unyielding and unbending like the candles themselves. Afterward Megan's father accompanied Megan down the aisle. Traditional vows were spoken.

Hazel was surprised when she felt a tear well up at the pronouncement of husband and wife. Her watery gaze followed the newlyweds as they walked down the aisle out to the lobby, where a greeting line soon formed. Photographers dodged in and out, clicking their cameras, seemingly everywhere all at once. At one point, Ben and Megan motioned for Hazel to come forward to be included in some family shots. She felt both awkward and honoured.

The reception was held a few kilometres away at a community hall, although it wouldn't start for another two hours. As the bridal party drove off to take photos amongst the manicured lawns and flowerbeds of Riley Park, Hazel wondered what to do with herself. Driving home would be a waste of gas, so she went straight to the community hall and parked. She proceeded to walk in the sunshine to a nearby coffee shop.

Just outside the front door, she abruptly noticed a small piece of wrinkled paper stuck in a shrub. She came to a halt. Since finding Praveen's receipt, Hazel seldom looked at the ground anymore, other than to keep herself from tripping. She didn't want to see any more receipts. She hadn't yet acted upon her receipt for the umbrella and didn't want to have to deal with any others. She could only handle one at a time.

For Pete's sake, I really have let this whole thing get way out of hand, she told herself. *And it's all so silly!*

Hazel walked past the receipt and entered the coffee shop. She hummed and hawed over the glass-covered display of donuts, but her mind stayed on the receipt outside.

While drinking her coffee and enjoying her maple-dipped donut, she thought more about the receipts. In the past nine months, she'd picked up five of them. She wished the number five carried scriptural significance—like the number three, seven, or twelve—that would allow her to end the game cleanly. In terms of the Bible, all she could think of were the five loaves of bread Jesus had multiplied. But did the number really matter? Her dismayed reaction at finding the sixth receipt seemed bad enough to convince her that the end had come. She would handle Praveen's receipt in some fashion, and that would be the end of the receipt game forever.

She asked God once again for help in deciding what to do with her upcoming vacation time. It had been two months since finding Praveen's receipt and she remained ambivalent. She didn't want to make a wrong decision. But if she was earnestly seeking to do God's will, God would guide her movements, right?

Anyway, she really did need to decide. Should she go to Scotland or have a staycation?

The thought of venturing overseas made her nervous. Flying such a distance wasn't the problem, but spending two weeks in such a far-flung locale was. She felt frightened. How overwhelming would it feel to be plunked down in the middle of Edinburgh—a foreign city, a foreign country, a foreign culture?

The fact that this receipt had been Praveen's meant something special, and she had a sense that she should finish what she'd started.

Staying home would be so much easier. It was a valid option. She had already made a mental list of all the things she could busy herself with. She'd bus downtown and see all the things she never had time to check out, such as the summer exhibits at the Glenbow Museum. She'd walk the river paths along the Bow, cross over on the Peace Bridge, and spend time in Prince's Island Park. With a takeout lunch in hand, she'd find a bench up in the three acres of the Devonian Gardens and walk around its tropical botanical loveliness. She'd even drive to the deep south of the city, to malls she rarely shopped at. Most importantly, she would arm herself with an assortment of good books.

But as comfortable as these ideas felt, they also made her feel like she was giving in—and giving up. The staycation plan rang of cowardliness.

She made her way back to the community hall having made at least one big decision. She would no longer pick up receipts. Praveen's would be the final one. All others would have to flounder in the wind or remain stuck in the snow. They were no longer her concern.

* * *

Hazel walked into the community hall under a balloon and ribbon archway of white. She found her name card at a spot near the head table. A metal lantern centrepiece sat in the middle of the table; the glass sides had been removed so a collection of roses could spill out. Hazel thought it looked marvellous.

Several of Megan's aunts and uncles had already been seated, and they welcomed Hazel warmly. The aroma of roast beef kept Hazel wishing the preliminaries would be short so they could all start eating. It was an enjoyable evening and Hazel loved everything about the dinner, which she ate way too quickly.

Afterward, the tables and chairs were shuffled toward the walls to allow room for a dance floor. The plates were cleared away to allow for desserts, coffee, and tea. Hazel sipped her coffee, watched people dance, and tapped her toes to most songs, recognizing a few. Sometimes she sat alone. Other times, someone from her table, tired of dancing, would sit and chat with her.

At one point while alone, Hazel saw Fran walking toward her. They hadn't connected all evening. It wasn't until Fran sat down and began talking that Hazel wondered how many glasses of wine she had drunk.

"Wow, what a day! Don't Ben and Megan make the perfect pair? You know, Hazie, I haven't told anybody this, but Ben might be getting tansferred... tans... transferred. Can you believe it?"

"Transferred?"

"Yep. Toronto. Do you know how far away that is? I'm going to miss Ben so much. And Megan... isn't she wonderful? How did she turn out so nice? Huh? With that... that battleaxe of a mother?" Fran's eyes became moist.

"Fran, I'd really like another coffee, and I bet you'd like one too."

Hazel began to get up, but Fran caught her sleeve. "You know, one minute I have my son here, and the next..." Failing to snap her fingers, she continued, "The next minute, my baby boy is gone."

"Well, Fran, if they do move... and it's not certain, right? But if they do, then you and Roger could go and visit. Do some travelling. Take in a Blue Jays game. You're both retired. You two used to travel around a bit. You need to get back to that."

"But I'm busy now. And travel's a hassle. You know, I once went up to Red Deer—"

"Fran, I mean travel to places further than just up the highway. You two should even try somewhere tropical."

Fran ignored her and carried on. "—to attend some conference or other. The hassle of booking into the hotel was..." Her arms expanded out wide. "I'm on my own, right? And what do they give me? A room with two beds." She thrust a peace sign with two fingers so close to Hazel's face that she couldn't focus. "Two beds. And I've got to pay extra for it."

"But I'm sure you got it straightened out."

"Oh, you bettcha. And cause I did that, you know, I still like Red Deer." Fran stared at her. "Anyway, Hazie, what do you know about travelling, huh? Nothin'. I mean you've been nowhere. Right?"

Hazel kept silent, choosing not to bring up her travels with Julie to Vancouver, or even her trips down to Montana. She'd travelled around the province for church retreats. It wasn't much travelling, but some.

"Fran, I wouldn't worry about Ben and Megan, wherever they settle," Hazel said. "I know you and Roger will visit, and I know you'll enjoy it. I would visit them in Toronto too, if they do move there. I mean, I like to travel a bit. In fact, I'm thinking of travelling this summer."

"What? Going where?"

"Overseas to Scotland."

The burst of laughter from Fran drew several people's attention.

"Hazie, Hazie, Hazie, you're funny." Her hand waved around the room. "Scotland's across the ocean. You know? A whole different place. You couldn't... you couldn't handle it."

"Well, it's not like I'm going to the Amazon rainforest."

Fran's outburst of laughter was even louder this time. "Hey, but you know..." Her finger stabbed Hazel in the shoulder. "You'd be good at the s'change rate. Their money—pounds, euros, whatever—you'd know *all* about it. Cause you're good with numbers. I really admire you, cause I'm not good with numbers. Good thing Roger is."

At the mention of Roger, Fran looked around the room with a look so glazed that Hazel didn't think it possible for her to focus on anything.

"Fran, you stay right here. I'll get us both a coffee and I'll get Roger to join us."

Hazel cut across the dance floor and found Roger, who stood chatting with Megan's father.

"I think you'd better check on Fran," Hazel whispered into Roger's ear.

Hazel returned with coffees and found Roger sitting beside Fran. Before she could even sit down, Roger turned his head toward Hazel.

"You're not serious about travelling overseas by yourself, are you?" he asked.

Her shoulders slumped as she placed the coffees down. She always expected Roger to be the voice of encouragement, but now he was the voice of Fran—a sober version.

"Yes, I am. I'm going to Scotland."

When she heard herself say those words with such finality, she felt terrified and triumphant. That's when she knew she had made her decision.

"Anyway, I'll just have this coffee and then I think it's time for me to say my goodbyes to everyone and get home," Hazel said. "You both have a fantastic daughter-in-law! It's been a wonderful evening. Ben and Megan look so happy together."

Farewell sentiments were exchanged and Hazel left the community hall. She didn't know whether she was more frustrated with Fran or with Roger.

Once home, she sat on her couch with the laptop open. She looked online for flight times and hotels close to the Royal Mile in Edinburgh. She got lost exploring the history of Scotland. Before she fell asleep, she had booked her flights and a hotel.

EIGHTEEN

Paris

WHILE STROLLING THROUGH the Tuileries Gardens in mid-June, Jean-Paul stopped in front of Auguste Rodin's statue of Eve; she stood in despair, covering herself in shame, a right and natural reaction to the sin of her disobedience. He walked further on, then paused to stare at Rodin's Adam. Both sculptures depicted their subjects with lowered heads. But Adam, with his head tilted and neck stretched out, looked utterly tortured. His arms hung awkwardly, appearing unnatural—stilted, not fluid. A disturbing statue indeed.

Adam, when first created, hadn't looked anything like Rodin's sculpture of course. He had once been a magnificent man. He was, as God declared, very good, but by his choices he became wretched. Jean-Paul held an odd affinity for this statue of Adam; through it, he saw himself as a wretched being.

The past few months had not gone well. Another target, this one in a side street in Salzburg, had looked toward Jean-Paul a moment before he pulled the trigger. Somehow Jean-Paul had made a faint sound while shifting his feet. That was all it had taken to destroy the excellence of his assignment.

Since then, he'd hesitated to accept any more assignments, at least for several weeks. Instead he lived at the rifle ranges, where his shots unfolded without any glitch. He would fire his rifle, hitting his targets exactly where he intended.

But peace eluded him. Any hint of physical awkwardness meant the death of his job. Why was this happening? How could he carry on?

Jean-Paul finally realized the truth of it all: he could not carry on. He had agreed to one upcoming assignment, a rather significant one that he declared to himself would be his last.

He moved away from Rodin's work. Glancing at the time on his phone, he walked toward the large open area in front of the Musée de l'Orangerie. Leaning against the concrete wall, a sculpture itself with its row of short bell-shaped pillars, he stared down at the Place de la Concorde and the Champs-Élysées, and over to his left, beyond the haze, he perceived the distant Eiffel Tower. His thoughts were many, some anxious and worried, others light and peaceful.

"Ah, Jean-Paul, looks like I caught you sight-seeing."

He turned. "*Bonjour, Maman.*"

He gave his mother a hug and kiss as they made their way past Adam and Eve along the Tuileries. She had suggested they meet there, to give them an opportunity to stroll through the gardens together before having lunch at a restaurant further down near the Louvre.

"I think the end of summer would be a good time to quit my job," he told her. "I've been thinking about it for the past several months. You know it's been a bit unpredictable, with me never knowing whether I'm coming or going."

"A bit?" Brielle interjected with a smile, as though she couldn't quite believe what she was hearing.

"But I feel ready for a change now. I'll have the summer to tidy things up, finish a few projects. It means I'll only have worked in the business two years." His hands flew up. "*Mais c'est la vie.* I've been thinking about how much I miss architecture."

He didn't honestly know whether he'd go back to architecture. In fact, he doubted he would, but he knew it would please his mother to mention it. She would worry less.

"You did seem to thoroughly enjoy that work," she remarked. "I suppose architecture won't be as profitable. But you are doing okay, *n'est-ce pas*?"

Jean-Paul thought about the near half-million euros he'd accumulated in several accounts. "It would mean less income for sure. But I've done okay. I know I'll manage."

They continued walking, their view dominated by the colourful carousel. It took Jean-Paul back to his childhood days, when life, although not without pain, had still provided simplicity, even carefreeness. He longed to be transported to those easier times, but at least he was making progress. He'd be free from his job soon.

He turned and noticed his mother studying his face very carefully, no doubt watching for worry lines and other signs of anxiety.

As for her, she seemed to bask in the sunshine.

"Once I'm finished, before I look for new work, I've had the idea to take a cruise," he added. "Maybe the Caribbean, with so many fascinating islands and great places to escape to and relax. Some cruises can last a week, but I was thinking something like a month." He paused. "And I'd like you to come with me."

"Come with you? On a cruise?"

Jean-Paul gave one of his rare smiles, knowing that the idea must excite her.

"Well! Jean-Paul, I don't know if I could handle a month away from Paris. A whole month on a ship?"

"*Maman*, you *do* get off the ship and go on excursions. Not every day, but most days. You explore an island here, a city there. I'll do some research and see what I can find. Maybe a cruise in September. It's time you saw life outside of Paris."

"I don't know about that. But it would be wonderful to spend time with you."

Before they reached the doors of the restaurant, his mother turned to him again. "You will be around this year for Bastille Day, won't you?"

"That's still a few weeks away," he replied with complete assurance. "But don't worry, I'll make sure I'm free. I've only missed a few. Another gathering at Marie's, right?"

Over lunch, they reminisced about the many Bastille Day celebrations they'd enjoyed over the years. Jean-Paul couldn't remember the last time they'd had such a pleasant lunch.

Outside the restaurant, they hugged each other and his mother remarked that she hoped he would put on some weight soon.

Well, it seemed to him the cruise would help with that.

• • •

Brielle walked across the bridge, her thoughts racing with excitement over the prospect of taking a September cruise with her son. She tried to picture herself in the tropics, strolling along beaches, sitting in the shade, reading magazines… standing on a ship, looking out at the vast waters with a low sliver of land on the horizon. What would she wear? Maybe a stylish V-neck tunic. But what style of hat? A bowknot straw hat or a floppy wide-brimmed one?

That afternoon, she taxied over to the Bon Marché department store. She wanted to get a start on shopping. After surveying the women's department, and leaving with a few wardrobe ideas, she walked toward Église Saint-Sulpice, a church she had attended many times for its magnificent organ concerts.

Brielle lit a candle and placed it in a line alongside others at the base of a statue of St. Peter. But it was to God whom she prayed. She believed neither Peter nor Mary was a match for the Father, Son, and Holy Spirit. She thanked the Lord several times for the changes she saw in Jean-Paul. She thanked God for such an exciting future.

She exited and walked past the grand fountain at the front of the church, a fountain she had never liked. It was called the Saint-Sulpice Fountain but was often referred to as the Fountain of the

Four Cardinal Points. Most people believed they were looking up at the statues of four church cardinals, but they would be wrong. The fountain's statues only represented bishops, those considerably lower in the Catholic hierarchy. The Fountain of the Four Cardinal Points simply indicated the four points on the compass. The apparent deception bothered her.

However, she loved the sound and sparkle of the falling waters. She watched it flow over the basins down to the four lion statues positioned at ground level. Their snarling mouths and bared teeth seemed to say that they too were angry at how easily a person could be deceived.

NINETEEN

Calgary–Edinburgh

ANTICIPATION HOVERED OVER the city during the first few days of July, with final preparations being made for the annual Calgary Stampede, dubbed the greatest outdoor show on earth. Calgary began to swell with tourists eager to enjoy ten days of rodeo, midway rides, and free pancake breakfasts. Even politicians would descend on the city from across the country, dressed in jeans, shirts and cowboy hats, to flip pancakes and casually, or sometimes not so casually, promote their platforms.

Hazel took little notice of any of it. She had a two-week vacation to prepare for.

On a Saturday morning, Hazel walked into a shopping mall nursing a large black coffee. She wore dangling dreamcatcher earrings and a T-shirt with jeans belted to show off the large brass buckle. She didn't look out of place as she leaned against several stacked bales of hay, although the smell of the straw competed with the strongly brewed coffee. Beside Hazel stood the life-sized cardboard cutout of a cowboy and cowgirl, their faces removed and ready for fun-seeking shoppers to stick their own faces through.

She was waiting for the magic hour of nine, when all the stores would slide back their accordion doors. At one minute to nine, she downed the remainder of her lukewarm coffee and entered the travel store. She was the first customer to peruse the store-wide sale.

Hazel felt unprepared for her adventure in every way. She wasn't a seasoned traveller and didn't know all about the travel paraphernalia available to smooth out a vacation and make it more enjoyable. It certainly hadn't taken long for Hazel to lose herself in the woes of trip-planning. She'd read of endless travel hazards, as well as solutions. Should she purchase a phone mount, or take the risk of going without? Should she wear compression socks on the plane, in case of poor circulation? Or an airplane foot hammock? Should she invest in an anti-theft cross-body bag? Why not also add a unique scarf with hidden pockets? What about suitcase trackers?

As she perused the aisles, her head swam with worry. There were far too many *what-ifs*. She needed more time to consider all the disastrous possibilities and calculate their probabilities.

Anyway, the current store's sale would last until Wednesday. She could always return. After all, the only items she absolutely required at this point were a bag and a carry-on suitcase.

She left with a small black suitcase on wheels, as well as a sturdy grey travel bag.

. . .

By the end of the first week of July, with the Stampede in full swing, Hazel sat in her office contemplating the fact that she had only three days before leaving for Scotland. She wore a plaid shirt and dark jeans, having dodged the square-dancing and street entertainment outside the building and doing her best to ignore the smell of pancakes and sausages.

That day, Maddie had dressed simply in jeans and a T-shirt.

"You look really good in plaid!" Maddie commented. "You normally dress so... so conservative. I guess soon you'll be surrounded by plaid everywhere once you get to Scotland!"

"Thanks, Maddie. I find plaid a little loud, but I suppose this shirt is okay. Anyway, Scotland has *tartan*, not *plaid*. Plaid, I suppose, is more of a North American thing. Tartan is more specialized, pertaining to Scottish clans."

"Well, it all looks the same to me!"

Hazel made her way to grab another coffee to take back to her desk, thinking about the difference between tartan and plaid.

I'm not buying a plaid umbrella, she thought. *Not some big, ugly checkered thing. I'm going to buy a tartan umbrella, sophisticated and classy.*

She had worked hard to foresee as many accounting problems as possible. The fewer issues left in the hands of Maddie and Mr. Lee, the better. She ensured they both had her phone number if they needed to contact her—about anything, absolutely anything.

"Please let me know right away if there are any issues," she said, occasionally forgetting about the eight-hour time difference. "Just email, text, or call and I'll get right back to you."

It felt really hard to go away, like leaving her child in the hands of a babysitter for the first time. She tried not to think of all that could go wrong.

She hadn't even left the city, and already she was looking forward to going back to work and sitting behind her desk, surrounded by security and predictability.

Hazel left her office on her last day, shirking the feeling that nothing would be quite the same upon her return.

Earlier that week, she had met up with Fran to hand over her spare apartment key. Fran had agreed to check on her place every four days, as stated in Hazel's insurance policy. She also agreed to retrieve her mail, flyers and all, and water the Boston fern. Fran mentioned that if she were too busy, Roger would do it.

Her sister also insisted that Hazel leave her flight and hotel details in case of emergency. Hazel wondered whether Fran really cared about her or just needed to feel a sense of control. In their phone calls and texts, Fran never wished Hazel a wonderful vacation. She offered no encouraging sentiments such as "Have a wonderful time, Hazel. I'll be praying for you. Take lots of photos."

"I still can't believe you're going," she said instead. "Are you sure you want to do this? I can't help but think this is bordering on recklessness. You know, Hazel, you've never travelled far, and certainly never on your own."

During her last evening at home, Hazel packed and repacked her suitcase and bag, finally getting it to an acceptable level of organization. When all was ready, she sat at her kitchen table and double-checked her financial accounts. All credit card and utility bills had been paid; no company would earn even a penny of interest where Hazel was concerned.

She updated her prayer journal as well, after reading it from start to finish. She felt encouraged by the accounts of her personal progress. She envisioned the "Adventure" column growing by many, many pages.

By the time she went to bed, Hazel had written almost an essay on the adventures of just preparing for travel.

* * *

On the morning of her flight, Hazel stood in the lobby waiting for a taxi. She often glanced down the hallway and thought about Praveen and how much she missed him. Wouldn't it have been wonderful to return home and tell him all about her adventures? This was all happening because of him and his receipt.

She felt like she was on a mission. She'd placed the receipt in a protective plastic card holder and tucked it away in her wallet.

For Hazel, her vacation began the moment she stepped into the taxi. At the airport, she remained unperturbed by lineups and hassles. After showing her passport one last time before boarding, she tucked it away next to her turquoise journal.

Throughout the day's flights—first from Calgary to Toronto, then from Toronto to Edinburgh—Hazel repeated a mantra of short sentences: *I'm on an adventure. God is with me. I can do this.*

When the overhead lights dimmed on her transatlantic flight, Hazel found that she couldn't sleep. She was too wound up. But she also couldn't get absorbed in the pages of a crime novel, because she hadn't brought one. Her reasoning at the time of packing had seemed ironclad: since she'd be experiencing her own adventure, she didn't need to escape into someone else's. She needed to live in the real world. Her own world. This was *her* life.

She pulled out her phone and played a few games instead.

● ● ●

Hazel arrived in Edinburgh at about ten o'clock in the morning, ready to implement her jetlag plan. Once at her hotel, she would unpack and immediately begin exploring. Nothing too strenuous, like hiking up to Edinburgh Castle. She just intended to saunter around, have an early dinner, then sleep around eight o'clock.

Walking through the airport, she followed the exit signs but eventually found it easier to just follow the flow of foot traffic. Once out of the security area, she bypassed the luggage carousels in search of doors leading to the taxis.

On the way, she came upon a wall holding a huge expanse of brochures and booklets in wooden slots. The sight almost took Hazel's breath away. She veered toward them, colliding with two men and their suitcases. Hazel apologized, then spent considerable time browsing the colourful information. She grabbed several tourist maps and hunted for specific brochures on cathedrals, castles, and museums. The pile of brochures, about twenty thick, found their way into her bag's side pocket.

Repositioning the bag on her shoulder, Hazel grabbed her suitcase and headed outside where she was greeted by cloudless skies and sunshine.

An official wearing a jacket and cap directed her to the next taxi in line. She'd wondered how difficult it would be to understand Scottish accents, but with each encounter she realized she could manage quite well. She understood most of the words of the chatty taxi driver and he quickly got her to her hotel.

The spacious lobby with its warm, tartan-patterned couch and accompanying sofa chairs gave Hazel a cozy Scottish welcome. The check-in went smoothly and Hazel's confidence reached new heights. She took the small elevator to the fifth floor.

She found the hotel room somewhat less splendid than the main lobby. It was small and compact, but also clean. From the swivel chair, tucked into a table, she had a view of brick buildings and large deciduous trees. Between the bed, chair, shelves, and ensuite, Hazel could navigate every feature of the room in just a few steps.

Soon Hazel had everything unpacked and felt settled.

Hazel stowed her extra credit card and cash in the room safe, following advice she'd read online. However, fears of the hotel burning down while she was out and about persuaded her to tuck her passport away in her purse's inner pocket.

The coffeemaker looked inviting, but Hazel resisted using it. She wanted to get outside, explore, and find a café. Adventure was calling! With several brochures in the side pocket of her purse, she left her room.

As soon as she closed her door, she heard a voice from down the hallway. "Hi, ye lassie. First time in Edinburch?"

She turned to see a man, about sixty years old and six feet tall. Strong build. Silver wavy hair. Deep voice. He appeared like a hero-type figure, a fisherman of the North Sea having stepped out of a seascape. Hazel noticed the toolbelt hung around his waist. In his left hand, he held a stepladder.

She struggled to respond.

"Hello," she ventured after a seeming eternity. "Yes, this is my first time here."

"And where might ye be from?"

"Canada."

"And what a fine country to come from. I'm George, by the way. Ye'll see me around walkin' the halls. Been workin' here for years. A resident ghost! And what might ye name be?"

"My name is Hazel."

"Ah, such a lovely name for a lovely lass. Well, ye have yourself a great day."

He tipped his cap and carried on down the hallway, whistling as if he whistled every day of his life, happy to be in his hotel haunt.

Hazel watched him walk the length of the hallway and disappear around a corner.

She felt the warmth of being noticed by someone. Someone of the male species. She wanted to hold onto that feeling. It reminded her of Bobby What's-His-Name when he'd approached her locker to chat on the first day of Grade Seven.

Her smile remained as she descended in the elevator and walked across the lobby. Not until she stood outside to consider one of the airport's tourist maps did her smile fade. Hazel had a perfect sense of direction—in Calgary. Without hesitation, she could point north toward the Arctic, south toward Mexico, east toward the prairies, and west toward the Rocky Mountains.

But here in Edinburgh, everything was out of whack.

When she figured out which way was north, she soon arrived at the famous Royal Mile. A series of adjoined three- and four-story buildings stretched down the street as a conglomeration of dark weathered brick. Occasional colourful signage attached to wrought iron protruded from these ancient structures, indicating pubs, giftshops, and cafés.

Hazel sauntered along the cobblestones packed with tourists and finally decided upon a café where a few tables and chairs overflowed out from its doors. In no rush, she sat for some time, feeling rather amazed.

Am I really here? Across the ocean? In Scotland?

The air smelled fresh and the slight breeze brought her a chill of excitement.

While waiting for her chicken sandwich, she studied the ancient stone, brick, and wood, fascinated by the centuries of history. It was so unlike the young, sprawling city of Calgary.

She watched families walk by, talking and laughing. Couples strolled hand in hand. Some passersby walked with a good stride, and she figured they must be locals. But they all had one thing in common: they were headed toward something and knew where they were going. They knew their next move. Even a mottled-grey cat, having slunk around a corner, sat for a few minutes to observe life only to jump a fence and disappear, moving on to other things.

Just then, a profound sense of loneliness descended upon her, and she felt anxious. How nice it would be to have a friend at her table, someone to chat with and discuss afternoon plans. She felt exhausted and oddly invisible. At first she blamed this on jetlag and feared returning to her hotel too soon, where she would be tempted to fall asleep.

She reminded herself that at least she did have a plan—a small plan. In fact, it was more than that. She had a mission to accomplish. She needed to follow through with the fifth and final receipt.

As she sat there, she thought it strange that she hadn't researched anything about the giftshop itself. Besides researching all the flights and hotels near the Royal Mile, she'd mostly concentrated on learning Scottish history, to feel prepared for such a trip and less ignorant.

If the giftshop was nearby, she could make her way over to it now. If it was way down at the other end of the Mile somewhere, she'd go tomorrow, after she'd had a good night's rest and somewhat recovered from the jetlag.

She dug out her phone and typed the words "Jedburgh Royal Gifts" into the search window. A series of photos immediately stole Hazel's attention and she browsed through the shop's lovely merchandise.

At last she clicked on the map—and realized that the store didn't appear to be on the Royal Mile at all. In fact, she couldn't figure out where it was.

She expanded the map, only to discover that the location indicator rested on a town called Jedburgh.

A town? Jedburgh can't be a town! It can't be, for Pete's sake!

The more she scrolled links associated with Jedburgh, the more she began to sweat. The giftshop was indeed in a town about eighty kilometres away, situated halfway between Edinburgh and the Scottish-English border, near Hadrian's Wall.

Hazel hurriedly retrieved Praveen's receipt from her purse. She even removed it from its plastic holder, as if to confront it head-on. Upon examining the printout for several minutes, she realized how she'd managed to make such a poor assumption. The first line read "Jedburgh Royal Gifts." The address, if you could call it that, followed with a simple "Edinburgh Rd." The third line simply read "Jedburgh." That was it, except the item purchased of course—a "trtn umbrlla" for six pounds.

How could she have been so careless?

It was an easy mistake to have made, she realized, recalling her conversations with Praveen. He had highlighted his time in Scotland, delighting especially in Edinburgh, walking everywhere from his hotel to the Royal Mile, which was in close proximity to everything: museums, castle, churches, and many giftshops.

Okay, so I've made a big mistake. What do I do now?

She found four different options for getting to Jedburgh from Edinburgh. She could drive there in an hour and a half, take the train in two hours, bike in six hours, or walk in seventeen hours.

Sure, I'll just take a day and a half to walk there and back, for Pete's sake.

Renting a car and driving on the wrong side of the highway was out of the question. The only reasonable alternative was to take the train. Besides, her research described Scotland's train system as superb. The train lines weaved all over the map from the south side of Edinburgh to a host of small towns, Jedburgh among them.

Well, that looks doable, I suppose, as long as I get on the right train. It will be a headache for sure.

As much as she wanted to accomplish her mission, she wasn't ready to explore the countryside. She felt it wise to give herself a few days in Edinburgh to acclimatize to the culture and get into a more relaxed and carefree frame of mind. Then she'd plan her little side trip.

With an afternoon to fill, she consulted her map and chose to wander down to the Writers' Museum. The street was a continual flow of people walking slowly by and often stopping to peer through the windows or consult their phones.

On her way, Hazel entered a clothing boutique, drawn in by the colourful window display of all things tartan—kilts, jackets, pants, and scarves. Upon entering, she realized this was not a tacky tourist trap. From her research, she knew that modern Scots wore whatever pattern and colour of tartan they liked. The old rules had become traditions. But she respected the fact that many Scots still chose their clan tartan, the colours that pertained to their heritage.

Hazel strolled by an array of kilts, then stopped at an assortment of scarves. Despite the exorbitant prices, she picked up several, allowing the soft silk to glide over her fingers. The purchase would be like an investment in her professional wardrobe.

Not having a drop of Scottish blood in her, Hazel chose what she loved. She pictured herself at her desk, a scarf of beige and black wrapped in classic fashion around her neck. The image gave her great pleasure.

The clerk wrapped the scarf in black tissue and placed it in a gold-coloured paper bag. Shopping had never given much of a lift to Hazel's spirit, as it did for others, like Fran—but it did today. She walked on with a confidence she'd been missing a half-hour earlier.

She turned off the Mile and soon found the museum. Carved in the stone archway above the door were the words "FEARE THE LORD & DEPART FROM EVIL—1622." Hazel stood back to capture it on her phone camera.

Smiling, she entered the museum, feeling excited to see a giftshop filled with books. Before exploring the worlds of Robert Burns, Robert Louis Stevenson, and Sir Walter Scott on the levels above and below, the cashier warned Hazel of the low ceilings and dim lighting. Complicating this were the varying heights of steps, sometimes quite dramatic. It turned out the steps had often been built this way to provide a type of alarm system against burglars. Only someone personally familiar with a house could easily bound up and down its stairs. A thief could trip and get caught. Hazel thought this clever, although it would hardly meet today's building codes.

After an unhurried hour taking in biographical information and appreciating the famous writers' books, desks, and personal items, she returned to the book shop. She envisioned herself back home, sitting on a park bench, reading something other than a murder mystery. Noticing a volume of Robert Burns' complete poetical works, she decided to purchase a copy. She felt content, even cultured, to have bought herself the souvenir. More importantly, a book was like a companion, and she hoped to feel less lonely.

She returned to the hotel, feeling she had accomplished enough for her first day. Immediately she placed her new, sophisticated scarf in the safe. She then picked up the Robert Burns book and opened it to a random page, expecting to read through a few poems. She landed on page 140 and read:

> While new-ca'd kye rowte at the stake, an pownies reek in pleugh or braik.[3]

Oh, for Pete's sake. There must be something here I can understand.

She jumped ahead two centimetres, bringing her to page 554:

> Now spring has clad the grove in green,
> and strew'd the lea wi flowers;
> the furrow'd, waving corn is seen,
> rejoice in fostering showers.[4]

---

[3] Robert Burns, *The Complete Poetical Works*, ed. James A. Mackay (Catrine, UK: Alloway Publishing, 1993), 104.
[4] Ibid., 554.

By the fifth stanza, her eyes began to close. The book slipped from her hand and tumbled to the floor.

Hazel jerked awake. Now fully alert, she knew she would have to do something else.

She took the elevator down to the lobby and approached the hostess of the hotel's restaurant, who had turned to survey the tables. She jumped when she heard Hazel's calm voice.

"I'm so sorry to startle you," Hazel said apologetically.

She soon occupied a table, enjoying a light supper of soup and salad. Afterward she remained in this pleasant restaurant to write in her journal. She questioned why she'd had that bout of loneliness earlier.

But for now she was in a better frame of mind. Even though she had made a big mistake with the receipt, at least she had a plan to deal with it.

She wrote about walking the Royal Mile, where for five hundred years kings and queens had proceeded from the Edinburgh Castle at one end to the Palace of Holyrood at the other. She browsed through tourist pamphlets, gathering ideas for how to fill her upcoming days.

Back in her room, after showering, she clicked through the television channels, often stopping at the BBC to take in world news. By seven-thirty, she had fallen asleep.

TWENTY

Edinburgh

WHEN HAZEL'S ALARM played a droning bagpiped tune at seven o'clock the next morning, she promptly rose. As she stood and did a few stretches, she found herself hoping to hear real bagpipes at some point in her vacation.

She pulled on her beige jeans and black cotton top. With a glance out the window to the grey clouds, she added her mustard-coloured cardigan and draped the black raincoat over her purse, ready to leave.

She had decided to walk further along the Royal Mile. Her map highlighted many other places to see, such as John Knox House, St. Giles' Cathedral, Palace of Holyrood, and plenty of giftshops and cafés in between.

Having realized her negligence to pray, she dropped her purse and coat on the bed and walked over to the window.

God, I thank you for this day. It should be a restful one, wandering around interesting sights and getting over jetlag. Back to full strength. I trust you to help me relax with this last receipt. I trust you to lead me to Jedburgh in a few days. Meanwhile, help me to just enjoy today.

She turned away from the window and, realizing her incomplete prayer, quickly mumbled, *In Jesus's name I pray, amen.*

When Hazel exited the elevator and entered the lobby, George waved from across the way and approached her. For a fleeting foolish second, Hazel imagined him saying something like "If ye have time today, I'd like to buy ye a coffee." George said nothing of the sort. He merely inquired about her plans.

Hazel wondered about the attention he gave her and then wondered about her attraction toward him. Was she suffering from severe loneliness, or perhaps culture shock?

She had no intention of ever telling him about her real mission in coming to Edinburgh in the first place. She felt he would certainly question her sanity.

"After breakfast, I'm going to explore the Royal Mile a bit more." She hesitated to say anything further. But when she caught his enchanting smile, she added, "I went to the Writers' Museum yesterday."

"Now there's a fine museum. True Scottish literature!"

They chatted for a while about Scottish authors and museums.

After a coffee and muffin at the restaurant, Hazel left the hotel. She appreciated the crisp and fresh morning air. At this hour, the city still held that quiet hum before the busyness of the day began in earnest.

She heard the click and turn of a key as a storekeeper opened her hair salon. Hazel then glanced across the street at the sound of a sandwich board being dragged across the stone and propped against the open door of a deli. Such sounds would soon go unnoticed as the streets filled with people, conversations, honking horns, and ordinary city bustle.

Hazel proceeded toward the Royal Mile, enjoying the fascinating history all around her. She noticed the skies growing cloudier and was glad to have brought her raincoat.

Once on the Mile, she began making her way down toward the John Knox House.

Along the way, Hazel noticed a tacky but fun-looking giftshop and entered to find the shelves overcrowded with knickknacks of all kinds. The rows of colourful shelves gave little allowance for customers to comfortably pass by one another. Hazel wasn't sure she'd want to be stuck here when business picked up.

While contemplating fridge magnets, Hazel stood near two other women whose conversation she couldn't help but overhear.

"Yes. I know! I mean, I understand the employees' issues, but at the same time I was going to visit my dad next weekend. He hasn't been well."

"Well, the last train strike lasted only a few days. So maybe this one will too. But somehow I'm not all that hopeful."

As the two women left the store, Hazel felt her desire to browse fridge magnets squashed by news of this train strike.

Next she noticed two women who appeared to be employees. The younger one, with blue hair and piercings, sorted through purses and wallets. She looked like every other young person back home.

Hazel chose to approach the older woman standing behind the cash register; she looked much as Queen Elizabeth once had, with hair sprayed into shape. She wore a sweater over a buttoned-up shirt, revealing a string of pearls.

She's old enough to know the city well, Hazel thought. *Maybe she's like George. Been here forever and knows everything about Scotland.*

"Excuse me, but I just heard something about a train strike?"

Queen Elizabeth responded. "Yes, it began aboot four days ago."

"Does that affect all trains? I was planning on making a trip down to Jedburgh."

"Well, dear, disruptions are everywhere. There's an app ye should download that shows current train times, which fer now will update ye on the strike news. It will tell ye which rail staff are strikin' and which routes are affected. From what I know, the lines to Jedburch and those places south aren't runnin' at all. But there's lots to do and see here. So where are ye from anyway?"

"I'm visiting from Canada."

"Well, welcome! I hope ye have a wonderful time here. What's in Jedburch fer ye to see?"

"I had a friend visit there once and thought I'd venture down there too."

"Well, looks like you'll have to stay in Edinburch fer some time."

Hazel held onto the counter's edge for support and began to perspire. Understanding that Queen Elizabeth could offer no further information, she thanked her and went back outside.

She felt stunned at how much darker the skies had grown in the last few minutes. She looked all around the Royal Mile, wishing Jedburgh Royal Gifts would be just across the way, or just down the block. The fun venture of buying an umbrella had now become a complicated task, maybe even an impossible one. She needed to gather her thoughts.

Rain began to fall. With no umbrella, Hazel pulled up her hood and walked away, as if needing to distance herself from the disappointing news.

The drops grew heavier. The sidewalks, still busy with tourist traffic, now blossomed with umbrellas. Within seconds the rain pelted down, prompting more umbrella openings. People quickened their pace toward buildings, and many pulled open doors to disappear inside.

Not thinking clearly, Hazel didn't return to the giftshop, a convenient place to find refuge. Instead she walked quickly, looking ahead rather than behind.

About half a block down the street, she noticed a colourful overhanging metal sign and entered Deacon Brodies Tavern. Those escaping the rain already filled the entryway and Hazel stood at the back of the crowd.

Eventually, a waitress led her past tables of chatty people to a small table for two. She removed her wet coat to let it drip from the back of her chair. She dried her hands on her cardigan and worked to calm herself down.

So far, Hazel had experienced nothing but friendliness in Scotland. Everyone came across as hospitable, and she expected that to continue with yet another cheerful waiter.

Instead she got Malcolm—at least, so declared his nametag.

"Wad ye want?" asked the server. He barely looked at Hazel and instead turned his attention toward two young women at a table across the way. He looked to be about their age, eighteen or nineteen.

Hazel waited until his eyes returned to her. "I'd like a menu, to start with."

He pointed to a plasticized piece of cardboard stuck behind the condiments, revealing a QR code. Again he looked over at the young women. Hazel looked too. One woman glanced at Malcolm with a smile, and he readily smiled back.

She waited again for his attention.

"Okay then," she said when he finally tore his eyes away from the woman. "What I'd like is a few minutes to look over the menu. And in the meantime, a cup of coffee—black, please."

Malcolm abruptly left, walking purposefully past the women.

Hazel watched him go. *Maybe it's young love, but that doesn't mean you have to be an insolent little twirp, Malcolm.*

She picked up the piece of laminated cardboard and glared at the QR code with disdain. It represented the main aspect of technology she disliked—the lack of a personal touch. No paper to hold in your hands. Nothing in a decent-sized print to easily read. Nothing to flip over in anticipation of more wonderful choices. Paper, even plasticized, had a warmth that a phone screen lacked.

Nonetheless Hazel retrieved her phone. The tavern's wi-fi was weak, adding to her frustration. She'd need to switch on her phone's data, which would cost her dearly.

Resolving not to let Malcolm worsen her already bad mood, she perused the menu on her screen. It tried to entice her into adventure: haggis, neeps, tatties, stovies, and cullen skink. But Hazel didn't want surprises, only security. And a place to think.

When Malcolm returned, he set down the coffee and Hazel gave her order of macaroni and cheese.

While waiting for her early lunch, she considered her situation.

She downloaded the app Queen Elizabeth had suggested, which had the official rail schedule, not the touristy one she had looked at earlier. Sure enough, no trains were currently running down to Jedburgh.

But what about buses? Maybe tour buses?

She could take a bus from a town called Tweedbank to Jedburgh, but that would require taking a train to Tweedbank...

There were always taxis. Would a taxi go cross-country, though? If they did, she figured the trip would cost a fortune.

She felt a growing anxiety, bordering on panic. She felt like Frodo: *I wish the receipts had never come my way. I wish I'd never picked them up.*

The prospect of not finishing the adventure made her feel like a cheater. Still, she could purchase a tartan umbrella... just not from the same shop as Praveen had. That would end everything.

What price was she willing to pay to finish this little game? With each forkful of macaroni and cheese, she entertained the idea of changing the rules.

Come on, Hazel, get a grip. Who says I have to go to the exact same store? Why am I putting myself through all this? It started out as something fun, and I need to get back to that.

When she concluded that it would be reasonable not to go to Jedburgh, she felt better. More relaxed.

As she finished off her lunch, her curiosity turned to the restaurant's namesake, Deacon Brodie. Who was he and what made him famous? Having been a deacon, she presumed he must have served the city of Edinburgh well in his day. She went online and searched.

Let's see, here we go... Deacon Brodie.

A webpage with the man's biography showed up in her search results. Apparently he had influenced Robert Louis Stevenson in developing the character of Dr. Jekyll and Mr. Hyde.

Oh dear, that can't be good.

She read on to learn of his innocent life as a tradesman and cabinetmaker by day. He even served on the town council. Part of his job involved installing and repairing locks, which gave him access to various places. By night, he went around robbing the homes to which he had gained insider knowledge, using his plunder to pay off gambling debts. Eventually he was caught, found guilty, and hanged in 1788, at the Tolbooth prison just beyond St. Giles' Cathedral.

Hazel paid her bill, almost feeling sorry for Malcolm, who had grown downcast after two young men joined the two women.

Well, Malcolm, I guess we're both having a bad day.

Back outside on the cobblestones, where the rain had lightened, Hazel continued her walk, unclear as to where she should go or what she should do. Walking helped her think.

Remembering that she hadn't turned off her phone data, she opened the device only to notice a text from Maddie. Nervous about a looming catastrophe at work, she opened the text.

"Is Mr. L shutting down business? Overheard him on phone say he's closing everything down next year!! Did you know about this? I can't lose my job!!! I just can't!!! Text me!!!"

For the second time that day, Hazel began to sweat.

He's not shutting down the business, she insisted to herself. *He can't be. Can he? He would have told me—wouldn't he? The company's not doing great, but business can't be that bad. Maybe Maddie misheard. Maybe that's all this is.*

She thought back to an incident a few weeks earlier. Mr. Lee had seemed preoccupied and she herself had been too busy with her vacation plans to give it much thought. But suddenly she began to recall conversations they'd had, considering them in a new light. Her memory even took her back to the beginning of January, when Mr. Lee had talked her into taking vacation time instead of pay.

He was worried, but I didn't twig onto it. I dismissed my concerns, even though I knew something wasn't quite right. Although it's possible for the business to keep going, maybe Mr. Lee doesn't want to keep going. After all, his arthritis is getting worse. His wife has retired.

Putting aside her fretting for a few seconds, she considered how to appropriately respond to Maddie. She didn't want to lie, but she also didn't want to cause further worry.

"I don't think you should worry," she texted. "You may have misheard or misunderstood what Mr. Lee meant. When I get back, I'll chat with Mr. Lee and sort everything out."

Before sending the text, she ensured the punctuation was correct and pressed send. Hazel returned the phone to her purse and began to walk nowhere in particular, although her job situation was the only thing on her mind.

What if she didn't have a job to return to? She couldn't imagine life without her job.

The lighter rain proved only a short reprieve. Moisture hung heavy in the air. Then a lightning strike startled Hazel, and the crack of thunder made her jump. She noticed only a few people now walking along the street.

The skies let loose.

Even people with umbrellas knew they didn't stand a chance and hurried through nearby doorways. Hazel looked back and realized she had walked a long way down from the restaurant.

In no time, she was drenched. Rain travelled down from her hood and onto her face, searching for any exposed opening in her coat to continue its course. Her shoes and jeans were soon equally soaked.

She hurried along, almost at a run, peering through the heavy rain for any welcoming doorway. Then she felt her upper body fall forward, her feet no longer touching the wet, uneven cobblestone. In quick reaction, she extended both arms to break the fall. Her hands absorbed the initial impact as she hit the ground and scraped along the contours of the stones. Her left cheek and forehead felt the impact. Her purse slid off her shoulders.

As if in a drunken stupor, Hazel struggled to get up, her efforts hampered by the torrents of rain gushing all around. Once up, she struggled to pick up her purse, ignoring the few brochures that had escaped from the side pocket.

In the misery of the moment, time came to a standstill. She found herself staring down at Praveen's receipt, the rain pummelling down and obliterating the print until the weakening paper separated.

She hobbled toward the nearest building and found shelter under a stone arch that curved over a wooden door complete with chains and padlock. The rain fell at an angle, though, continuing to hound her.

With a trembling hand, she steadied herself. She looked down at the blood running along her palm and between her fingers, diluted by the rain. Her left knee hurt, but she didn't bother examining it.

Through the downpour, she looked both ways along the street. The Royal Mile had become the Empty Mile. And to Hazel, the rain had become a merciless force in an overwhelming and inescapable situation. In fact, it all became too much. Despite the rain dripping down her face, she knew she was crying, for the tears were warm.

After a moment, she reasoned that she might as well make her way down to any door that would open. Any door at all. It could be a bar, brothel, or bingo hall—she didn't care. After all, she couldn't get any wetter.

As she walked, Hazel noticed what looked to be an open public square and the bleary shape of an umbrella. She limped toward it, like following a beacon, pausing once to notice that the building soaring above her was St. Giles' Cathedral. Feeling more tears, she painfully made her way toward the church's sanctuary, muttering to herself.

"Stupid, stupid rain…"

TWENTY-ONE

Paris

DESPITE THE FORECAST of heavy rain, Brielle and Marie still met for lunch at a restaurant along the Champs-Élysées, days prior to Bastille Day. The rain was such that Brielle couldn't help but talk about it when they first sat down.

"I heard there are to be heavy rains across almost all of Europe."

"Not to worry, Brielle," Marie replied, seemingly aware of her friend's fear of floods. "The rain is supposed to stop tonight, at least in Paris. I believe the forecast looks good for Thursday. And that's what matters, *n'est-ce pas?* The city has four days to dry out."

"You're right. There's no need to worry." Brielle dismissed the rain, or at least did her best to ignore it.

Instead she shared her good news with Marie.

"I have some wonderful news about Jean-Paul. He's retiring from this silly marketing job. I can hardly believe it. In a couple of months, he said. And Marie, I can't help but think that my prayers made a difference. I really feel they have. And he wants to take me on a cruise, somewhere warm like the Caribbean."

Both women ordered entrées and got deep into a discussion of what life would entail on a cruise ship, and what one should wear.

Before going their separate ways, they went over their plans for the upcoming Bastille Day celebrations.

Marie had reviewed the orders she'd placed and their delivery times—pastries from this pâtisserie, and breads and other pastries from that boulangerie. The best of the best. Cheeses and wines had already been purchased, leaving only a few things on her to-do list. She told Brielle about the extra help she'd recruited to come over and ensure her palatial apartment was spotless.

Both women had been raised to celebrate the country's Fête Nationale, marking the anniversary of the 1789 storming of the Bastille prison—and to celebrate it with great flair.

Brielle had also raised Jean-Paul to know about the importance of the French Revolution, as well as the need to celebrate it.

The annual celebration on July 14 at Marie's apartment had become a lavish affair where friends and family gathered with great anticipation. Jean-Paul had attended since his twenties. Her sprawling living room could easily handle more than twenty guests for a decadent breakfast. Some guests preferred to overflow onto her balcony, where they could be surrounded by cushioned chairs and an array of potted cedars. The balcony overlooking Rue Vernet guaranteed a great view of the aircraft flyover. And being situated only a block from the Champs Élysées provided easy access to the military parade. In the afternoon, everyone would disperse to other parties and concerts, echoing the cry: "*Vive le 14 juillet!* Long live the fourteenth of July!"

As was their tradition, Brielle, Marie, and several others would make their way over to their friend Claude's nearby apartment. From his vantage point, they could watch the phenomenal display of fireworks from the Eiffel Tower that lit up the skies for half an hour.

Brielle remembered how much Jean-Paul had enjoyed everything about Bastille Day as a young adult, and even now in his forties. She imagined the fun they would all have.

"You are sure Jean-Paul can make it this year?" Marie asked as if reading her mind. "You know he hasn't been to my place, nor Claude's, for three years."

"Of course he will. He promised. *Pas un problem.* Those were his words to me. He has a meeting, or something, but says he'll be back before Thursday."

Even though good changes were coming, Marie couldn't seem to help but voice her frustrations. "Well, let's hope he does show up. People always ask, 'How is Jean-Paul doing? What has he been up to?' It'll be good for him to be here and give his own answers!"

"He said he'd be here, and I have no doubt he will. We talked the other day before he left for the airport. I can't wait for his job to finish up. From now on, he'll be in Paris most of the time again."

"*C'est bon.* Where has he gone off to this time?"

"Not far. Just to Edinburgh."

ANSWERED PRAYER

Ask and it will be given you...
—Luke 11:9

TWENTY-TWO

Edinburgh

ST. GILES' CATHEDRAL in Edinburgh was the type of building most tourists would stop to admire before entering, to take in its structural beauty. Hazel had to assume they'd stare up at the gothic architecture and snap photos. Some might notice the carved figures on either side of the stone archway and appreciate the designs and glorious colours of the stained-glass windows.

But not in a downpour.

She made a stumbling beeline toward St. Giles', crossing West Parliament Square in front of the church. She barely remembered that this was the location of the old prison where Deacon Brodie had been hanged in the 1700s. She didn't have time to fully take note of the towering statue of Walter Francis Montagu Douglas Scott either.

Hazel kept her head low, focusing on the wet pavement she hobbled over—and when she reached the entrance archway, she painfully pulled open the heavy door.

She stood inside the cathedral, allowing water to drip off her raincoat onto the large rectangular entry mat. As she walked deeper into the structure, her eyes adjusted to a different kind of darkness from the gloom outside. Stone arches soared above her, supported by ancient pillars. Between them hung ornate lights emitting a golden glow. The building exuded warmth despite its grand interior.

Row upon row of wooden chairs filled most of the floor, right up to the distant altar. The light-coloured wood and wicker welcomed her.

Hazel observed only a smattering of people in the sanctuary, some sitting, others standing and looking upward. A few strolled around.

She limped forward, not sure where to go.

For a flicker of a moment, she recalled her conversation with Praveen back in October, when he'd talked about the cathedrals of Europe and Hazel had pictured herself walking through one and imagining it as the ultimate adventure.

Conscious of how she must look, she sought to become less visible—invisible, if possible. Hazel wanted to find the ladies washroom, to somehow improve her pathetic appearance. Feeling weak, however, she reconsidered and slowly headed toward a chair.

On her way to reach that chair, Hazel noticed booklets and pamphlets in her peripheral vision, nicely stacked on a wooden table. Despite her pain, she veered toward them and picked one up, a church bulletin left over from the service that morning.

It's Sunday today. I completely forgot.

She felt a touch of comfort in holding a church bulletin, like bumping into an old friend. A sense of connection with years long past. She marvelled at how substantial it was—six pages long. Certainly her church had never printed a six-page bulletin.

With bulletin in hand, she finally reached a row of chairs.

She shivered as soon as she sat, feeling her damp clothes cling to her skin. She took off her raincoat and placed it on the chair beside her. Out of the hundreds of empty chairs, she hoped no one would choose to sit in these chairs afterwards, at least not until they'd had a chance to dry.

She felt such relief to sit and rest. Besides an oncoming head-ache, she knew a bruise would soon emerge on her forehead. It might even become a large goose egg.

She retrieved a tissue from her purse to wipe her bloodied hand. Both hands had landed hard, but only one had started to bleed. Thankfully, the scrape on her cheek wasn't deep enough to draw blood. The pain in both knees, though, drew her attention to a small tear in her jeans, at her left knee. After dealing with the necessary bleeding, she remained sitting, as if in a trance.

Maddie's text replayed over and over in her mind and she internalized the words as if they were her own: "I can't lose my job!!! I just can't!!!"

As she considered life without her job, her sense of security plummeted and she broke down into tears. She looked every bit the repentant sinner, her hands gripping the back of the chair in front of her and her head resting on outstretched arms. She no longer cared what she looked like, nor what others might think. She no longer cared about receipts. Her only thought was about her uncertain future.

Eventually she sat up and reached for her purse to retrieve another tissue. She looked around, resting her bleary eyes on a nearby stained-glass window. The coloured panes depicted a shep-herd carrying a sheep; its red and orange hues made her feel warm and at peace.

The Lord is my Shepherd, she recited. *I shall not be in want.*

She fumbled to open the soaked, slightly bloodied bulletin and began reading a series of verses printed there.

> Hear my prayer, O Lord, and let my cry come unto thee. Hide not thy face from me in the day when I am in trou-ble; incline thine ear unto me: in the day when I call answer me speedily. (Psalm 102:1–2, KJV)

Like the psalmist, she too longed to be heard by God, for him to turn his ears toward her, and for her to experience his response and help. She felt overwhelmed, not only physically with aches and pains, but trapped by panic.

She continued reading.

And I say unto you, Ask, and it shall be given you; seek, and ye shall find; knock, and it shall be opened unto you. (Luke 11:9, KJV)

The next passage was among her favourites:

Be careful for nothing; but in every thing by prayer and supplication with thanksgiving let your requests be made known unto God. And the peace of God, which passeth all understanding, shall keep your hearts and minds through Christ Jesus. (Philippians 4:6–7, KJV)

She whispered her plea: "Jesus, you say to ask and it will be given to me. That you'll answer my prayers. The answers don't have to come speedily, but I would really like to know your peace speedily. So I pray for your guidance in this sudden mess. But what would I do without my job? I've been there so long. What would I do? And how would I manage without a paycheque?"

After several minutes, she reasoned that she needed to come to terms with the inevitable and trust God for her future.

"I want to follow your plan, and that may not include me working at Evergreen anymore. Help me to accept this, if the news is true. Help me to trust you for all my needs."

She thought about all the money she'd spent so far on this vacation. Money that she probably should not have spent. She shook her head thinking about the expensive scarf in the hotel safe and did a quick calculation of the current market price of her mutual funds.

Then she thought about George—not the hotel maintenance man, who she thought had winked at her as she crossed the hotel lobby that morning, but George Müller, the writer who'd referred to her as his *beloved reader*. He had lived under endless pressure to help hundreds of orphans and had concluded that he would cope by praying about every little thing, and he always expected God to answer, receiving necessary provisions and experiencing miracle after miracle.

He certainly wasn't wealthy with a stash of stocks and bonds, she recalled. *He relied on God.*

She remembered what he'd written about people getting old and their fears about having to go into the poorhouse. Whatever a poorhouse was, it sounded dreadful.

She also thought about getting another job and how hard it would be at the age of fifty-five. What if she couldn't find one? What if, after she'd gone through all her savings, she had to move into Fran's basement?

I'd rather die.

Poignant words from her pastor's sermon series came to mind: "Prayer is about relationship. A relationship with God. He must be the centre of one's life." With open hands, she simply offered herself up to God, surrendering everything about her uncertain future.

Within range of her hearing, an older couple stopped to chat with a minister in robes. The minister's accent held little Scottish cadence and Hazel was able to understand everything he said. His voice reminded her of Mr. Rogers, emitting a calm over the whole neighbourhood.

"Yes, St. Giles' often serves as a welcomin' refuge," the minister said. "Rain or shine, we get visitors from around the world daily. Tourists are always part of our congregation, whether they are in the congregation or just popping in durin' the week. In each service, we include a prayer for those visitin', for everyone comin' through our doors. There are some church bulletins near the door. Help yourself and enjoy your visit."

He politely excused himself and headed up toward the altar with a slight bow.

With this, Hazel remembered that she sat not only in an historic tourist attraction, a place of the past, but a functioning meeting place for the present. This was a place for a congregation to gather.

She wondered how old the building was and how many innumerable church services had been held under its stone arches.

Hazel left her historical ponderings to focus on the minister's words. It was amazing to think that before she had even come through the door, people this morning had already prayed for her. She was struck by how welcoming the church was and felt accepted, able to freely occupy the space she sat in. No one was about to ask her to move along. She was meant to be here.

Aching muscles had settled in, though, and she doubted she could have moved even if someone asked her to.

Hazel sat for quite a long time, lost in thought. She still felt sore, chilled, and tired, but in her heart she felt light, no longer in a state of panic. She had surrendered her overwhelming burdens to God and had nothing left to do now but trust.

She looked around at the array of organ pipes, side pillars topped with carved clusters of flowers, and more stained-glass windows, still beautiful even without sunlight streaming through them.

"Ask and it shall be given you," she whispered. "I want to trust you, Jesus, to answer my prayers for guidance, for provision, for a full life. I trust you. I trust you."

Hazel longed to get back to her hotel room. The idea of taking a shower and putting on dry clothes sounded glorious.

She rose from the chair, feeling every cut and bruise.

On her way to the washroom, someone opened one of the main doors and Hazel shot a glance out at the grey skies. Like Noah in the ark, she wondered whether the rains had stopped, whether it was safe to exit. The skies had improved a little, perhaps looking less dark.

In the ladies' room, Hazel spent considerable time combing through her wet hair, applying a touch of lipstick, and readjusting every article of clothing. She ensured that all signs of blood were gone. Her cheek showed signs of having been grazed, however, and she could do nothing but stare at the bump that had formed on her forehead.

In giving herself one last look in the mirror, she smiled. She liked the ordinary person, albeit injured and haggard, looking back at her.

She opened the church door, knowing she would come back sometime in the coming week to explore more of the incredible building. The solid mass of rainclouds had broken up, although they still gathered dramatically in the distance. She stopped to appreciate the beauty and take a few photos. Patches of blue sky were now mixed with the huge cumulus clouds. It didn't look like it would rain anymore, at least not for a while.

Normal life had once again resumed on the streets of Edinburgh. As Hazel made her way back to the hotel, though, she was brought up short by the sudden boom of cannon fire.

She wasn't the only one. A woman walking past Hazel noticed the confusion on her face and explained.

"That'll be the One O'Clock Gun," the woman said in passing. "It's a cannon firing from the Edinburgh Castle. Happens most days. Been happening for over a hundred years now."

"Well, thank you," Hazel called before the woman got out of earshot.

It's only one o'clock. Early afternoon? My goodness, it feels like it should be midnight.

On her way back to the hotel, Hazel remembered the destruction of Praveen's receipt. How had that happened? Hadn't she put it back in her purse? But she couldn't remember returning it to its plastic holder. She must have shoved it into her coat pocket, upset about having to head to a town called Jedburgh.

Anyway, she no longer had the receipt. That little piece of paper, so instrumental in directing her across the ocean, was no more.

Maybe it's a sign, she thought. *A confirmation. The receipt is no more, and so is my journey to Jedburgh.*

When she came upon a random giftshop, she knew what she needed to do. She chose an umbrella. Praveen had paid six pounds for his in Jedburgh, and Hazel paid eleven in Edinburgh. She chose a black one, since it would go with everything. Chic and classy.

It doesn't have to be tartan, she reminded herself. *It can be whatever I want it to be.*

She considered what a simple task she had just undertaken, so simple and freeing. How silly it had been to think she had to go to the exact store!

As she paid, various boxes of shortbread cookies on display near the cashier caught Hazel's eye. She bought two small boxes.

If nothing else, at least I'll bring back something for Roger and Fran, Ben and Megan. I'm on a shoestring budget now, so this will have to do. No more souvenirs. I'm done.

She left the store feeling accomplished, having truly freed herself of the burden of Praveen's receipt. She also felt like a boy scout—prepared, should the rain come again.

Once in the hotel lobby, Hazel headed straight for the elevator, hoping not to run into George. She couldn't hide her cuts and bruises and knew it would be impossible to completely shake off her drowned-rat appearance. She could hardly wait to stand in a hot shower and dress in clean, dry clothes.

While waiting at the elevator, she encountered a handsome middle-aged man. He looked like a tourist, casually dressed with a black backpack slung over his shoulder. She thought about saying a simple hello, but then, remembering how she looked, thought better of it. Besides, the man seemed preoccupied with his phone.

They entered the elevator and Hazel watched the man push a button. It glowed green, indicating the third floor. Since he didn't bother asking what floor Hazel wanted, she reached across, feeling a few aches, and pressed the number five.

The elevator ascended quietly. Hazel only heard the sound of the man tapping on his phone as he leaned into the corner. He then made his exit, with Hazel watching him as the doors closed.

She believed he was indeed a tourist, but she couldn't decide whether he was rude, preoccupied, or both.

TWENTY-THREE

Edinburgh

HAZEL SPENT SEVERAL minutes turning the hotel bathroom's shower handles every which way, trying to regulate the water temperature. Eventually she enjoyed her well-earned shower.

She then slept for an hour, in dry clothes and her cuts and scrapes attended to. The peaceful afternoon passed her by with the television turned on in the background.

Before dinnertime, Hazel took the elevator down to the restaurant. George was leaving for the day and brightened up when he saw her in the lobby.

"Hello there, Hazel. Hope ye had a good day."

"Yes, I did. Thank you, George."

A look of curiosity crossed his face when he noticed the bruise welling up on her forehead. Despite her best efforts at disguise, it poked out from between the brown strands of her hair.

"What sights did ye see?"

"I walked around the Royal Mile again. Spent time in St. Giles' Cathedral—well, the rain kind of drove me there. Oh yes, Deacon Brodie's—had a nice lunch." She noticed him looking more intently at her face and felt obliged to explain. "I slipped on wet cobblestone."

"Thought maybe ye got into a fight with someone at Brodie's! Sounds like ye need a walkin' guide." George hesitated, then added, "Well, Hazel, ye have a pleasant evenin. And take care of yeself."

"I'll certainly do that."

He gave her another wink and proceeded to the main doors.

Hazel's smile stayed in place as she crossed the lobby, all the while imagining another exchange with the man: *Why yes! I'd love to have coffee with you, George. You mean right now? How wonderful!*

She approached the restaurant, where the hostess noticed her from a distance. Once seated, she browsed the menu. She wanted to embrace the adventure, but not quite to the extent of ordering haggis.

While waiting for her dinner of smoked salmon, taters, pickled shallots, and red kale, Hazel took out her phone as well as a stack of pamphlets. She searched for something to do that evening, not wanting to give in to her injuries by doing nothing. She wanted to keep busy but also relax. Something not too taxing, considering her aches and pains.

She felt happy and at peace, having given her concerns over to God in faith. And it seemed she could once again hear adventure calling to her. After all, she had accomplished the task of buying an umbrella in Edinburgh. The rest of her vacation now stretched before her.

God will take care of me, she recited like a mantra. *I will be fine.*

She soon settled on an historical walking tour that didn't appear to be too extensive. "Suitable for all ages," the brochure claimed. Walking around might be the best thing for her.

Using her phone, she secured a reservation for the tour.

Hazel finished her meal with a slice of fruity Dundee cake, thinking it a good idea to energize herself for the tour ahead. It was so delicious that she struggled to refrain from ordering seconds.

• • •

The clouds had gathered in the west, having been ushered off centre stage, replaced by a sky of emerging stars. Even though the evening looked pleasant, Hazel slipped her new compact umbrella into her purse before making her way to the start of the guided walking tour. At dusk, she stood by a round kiosk not far from St. Giles' Cathedral. Wet paper advertisements barely clung to the kiosk. Others, having been plasticized and better anchored, had a chance of survival. In their disorganized arrangement, they amused Hazel while she waited.

When she heard a family approach with their two young rambunctious boys, Hazel turned to watch, relieved to know she wouldn't be the only one on the tour. The boys took turns jumping out from behind one of their parents to call out *boo* to the other. Immediately Hazel grew suspicious. Kids wouldn't be that excited about history, she realized, but they would be about ghosts.

Two other couples arrived, one in their thirties and the other elderly, ahead of a group of three men in their twenties, loud and energetic. Just then Hazel noticed a young, heavyset woman dressed in an ankle-length black robe. Her well-worn boots scuffed along the cobblestone. A wig of white hair billowed out around her head and thick bunches fell to her waist like octopus tentacles. The tour guide had arrived.

No one stood beside Hazel, but if they had, they would have heard her mumble, "Oh for Pete's sake, this *is* a ghost tour."

The woman smiled and introduced herself as Mystic.

Well, of course you are. Hazel knew she needed to curb her sarcasm.

The group gathered around Mystic, who proceeded with a few administrative duties. She was as energetic as she was eccentric. In a bubbly voice, she asked questions of each member in the group.

"What are yer names? Where are ye from? Is this ye first time here?"

Then she dispensed a brief history of Edinburgh. She led the group past St. Giles' Cathedral, careful to prevent collisions with other evening tours led by equally distinguishable guides.

Along the way, Hazel did a tally. *Thirteen of us, perfect for a ghost tour. Good thing I'm not superstitious.*

With each step, Hazel's appreciation for Mystic grew. The guide knew her material well and welcomed comments and questions.

"Candlemaker Row was named after the candlemakers who set up their shops here in the sixteenth century," Mystic explained as they embarked on the row in question. "They were extremely busy, with the ongoin' production o' candles. Back then, candles provided the only source o' light. Because they used tallow, which is leftover animal fats from butchers, the makin' o' candles was a smelly business, often producin' a real stench. No one would want to live downwind o' the candlemakers. Ye can imagine the ongoin' disputes."

Hearing these amusing stories boosted Hazel's excitement, despite her sore and tired body. The material was interesting and informative. She enjoyed the walk and the chance to leave behind the earlier events of the day.

A good choice for a tour, if I do say so myself.

They approached Greyfriars Kirkyard, which, prior to being a Franciscan monastery, had become a burial ground on the order of Mary Queen of Scots. At the entrance, a large sign set in concrete blocks, and old enough to match the surrounding gravestones, greeted them. The words informed passersby of sites within the cemetery they were about to walk past. It included an acknowledgement:

GRAVES OF MANY SCOTSMEN AND CITIZENS OF EDINBURGH OF WHOM SOME OF THE MOST IMPORTANT ARE…

Nineteen names followed. After taking a few photos, Hazel wondered why these people had been chosen. There must have been many others, just as worthy. She supposed it probably had to do with politics, money, and nepotism. She read of an historian, a caricaturist, and a mathematician. Only one name belonged to a woman; she had founded a school.

Having read every word and captured the sign with her camera, Hazel turned to discover that she stood alone in the vast cemetery filled with tombstones, shrubs, stone walls, paths, and hundreds of buried skeletons. She didn't see anyone along the path she believed the tour group would have taken. How quickly the twilight had ebbed and the skies grown dark.

A noise in the opposite direction made her turn and Hazel noticed movement far off to her left. The shape of a person dropped out of sight behind a copse of trees but then popped up again.

Hazel, get a grip. It's just a person walking by. Footsteps on gravel. As simple as that.

She felt on edge as the older of those two boys from earlier came bounding up a short set of stairs, arms spread out as though pretending to fly. He came running toward her, exuberant to be free of the adults but still protected by their presence just around the corner of a stone wall.

Hazel realized the boy was Mystic's chosen sheepdog to round up strays. She proceeded toward the rest of the tour group, doing her best to keep up with the boy.

Mystic smiled when Hazel and the boy returned. Without skipping a beat, the tour guide spoke of the plights of the men martyred beside the stone wall, as well as the monument commemorating the event.

They next stopped near the Covenanters' Prison, where Mystic warned everyone to be aware of ghost sightings, strange lights, and extrasensory perception. Hazel saw nothing and felt nothing other than an appreciation for the fascinating, well-preserved Scottish history she was learning about.

The walking didn't bother her, nor the fact that she always brought up the rear; she enjoyed being led and informed. She thanked God for bringing her to a place where she could enjoy herself both emotionally and spiritually.

Once through the graveyard, the tour continued along ancient streets. Mystic shared stories that went back as far as the 1600s, each one involving witches, torture, bloodshed, and ghosts. Hazel much preferred learning about candles.

The group turned off Cowgate and proceeded to Niddry Street, lined with short stone buildings. They stopped at a particular door which Mystic unlocked with a key she produced from her pocket. The bronze plaque beside the door read *The Caves*; above it, another plaque read "HE WHO IS WITHOUT MATHEMATICS SHALL NOT ENTER."

What a curious saying, she thought. *I don't know about anyone else, but I certainly have mathematics.*

As if reading her mind, Mystic explained that the words reflected an Enlightenment saying, "Let no one ignorant of geometry enter here"—which still didn't explain much.

The group followed Mystic down a set of stone stairs that took them underground into a series of caves. Each step produced a stab of pain, but Hazel persevered.

Before long, they stood in the middle of a cave while Mystic shared the history of the place. These caves had served as homes for the poor, horse stables, and storage rooms for whiskey. She told still more ghost stories and gruesome details of torture, ending with a warning that the caves of Edinburgh were the most haunted of all places.

Hazel felt uncomfortable and couldn't dismiss the thought that something awful had indeed happened here. She dismissed the ghost stories but didn't know what else to believe. It was hard to separate fact from fiction.

If these cave walls could talk, I would not want to listen.

She'd had enough of Scotland's bloody and horrifying history and looked forward to returning to her hotel room. And sure enough, they quickly made their way out of the caves and back to their starting point on the Royal Mile.

As the tour group began to disband, Hazel asked Mystic about a large building they'd passed near the beginning of the tour. Its modern light-coloured finish had made it stand out from the surrounding structures of dark stone and brick.

"That's the Scottish Parliament buildin'," the guide informed her. "I believe they have daily tours. Free, I think."

Hazel thought that a tour through the twentieth-century Parliament would be a good change of pace, on two accounts. Firstly, she would be indoors with no fear of being caught in another downpour. Secondly, this tour would include all the fascinating history she wanted without the frightening stories of martyrs and weird, mystical happenings.

Although I suppose I'll hear plenty of politics, she thought with a chuckle. *That can be scary enough!*

She thanked Mystic, complimenting her on her historical knowledge and interesting presentation.

In the growing darkness, many pedestrians continued taking in the sights. But Hazel made her way back to the hotel, where she researched Parliament and booked a free tour for ten o'clock the next morning.

Sitting on the bed, she sorted through the vacation receipts she had accumulated so far, most coming from restaurants. She then sorted through her pamphlet collection and organized them into piles. Those of no interest were stacked to the left and would be recycled. Those which held some interest were placed in the middle. And like seed landing on good soil, Hazel placed to the right those which were absolute must-sees.

The hefty church bulletin she had picked up at St. Giles' Cathedral found its place to the far right, in a category all its own, for it had already become one of her most valuable papers.

She yawned throughout her organizing task, but soon each piece had found its proper place.

. . .

Jean-Paul didn't need to do much to get settled. He'd only be in this hotel one night before flying back to Paris the following day.

The thought of taking a walk through the fresh air seemed inviting, so he went outside and began walking the streets, heading toward nearby Greyfriars.

So far the Edinburgh job had been incredibly disorganized, causing great stress. He'd already determined that this would be his last job—ever. He could hardly wait for it to all be over. He looked forward to taking that cruise.

As he walked across the graves, he accidentally dropped his phone and bent down to pick it up. Was this another sign of his increasing carelessness? His growing worries refused to disappear.

All evening, he'd been awaiting confirmation of the job's details. Finally, the text came through. Everything seemed to be falling into place.

Detecting movement to his right, he watched a young boy run and jump toward a woman, maybe his mother, aunt, or grandmother. He couldn't tell which, but they both disappeared down a path.

Somehow the sight of them brought to mind his own mother. He was excited to take her on a cruise while she remained in good health. He smiled again, recalling her excitement. And in the meantime, he could look forward to attending the Bastille Day celebrations at Marie's apartment.

Jean-Paul followed a path that took him around a stone wall. Spotting an exit, he decided to take it as another tour group made its way through.

Wanting to remain obscure, he decided to head back to the hotel. He had gotten what he wanted—fresh air and a walk. Now he just needed a good night's sleep.

TWENTY-FOUR

Edinburgh

WHEN HAZEL AWOKE, she lay in bed reliving the previous day—a nightmare of a day that had at least ended well. She wanted to continue feeling at peace, without letting worries about the future hound her.

"Jesus, help me keep you in the centre," she prayed before her feet even hit the floor. "And help me not to worry about losing my job. Whatever happens, you'll work everything out. I want to enjoy this vacation day. Help me to cast all my cares on you because you care for me."

She dressed in dark jeans with a white cotton shirt and beige cardigan. Her black flats had dried out and would be comfy for her walk around Parliament. It was a relaxed tourist look for a relaxing day.

Surveying the skies from her window and seeing nothing but blue, she slipped her new umbrella into her handbag anyway, as if holding onto the symbol of her freedom from receipts and her preparedness to take on the day no matter what might happen.

The walk from the hotel to a nearby café triggered the aching in her knee, but Hazel did her best to ignore it and carried on with a slight limp. Having seen Scotch eggs on every menu since her arrival, she finally ordered one for breakfast. The hard-boiled egg, wrapped in sausage meat, covered in breadcrumbs, and then deep fried, tasted exquisite, especially with the chutney.

As she ate, she looked over a map. Too many attractions clamoured for her attention. There was too much to explore. How easily she could miss seeing a must-see tourist site. Upon returning home, she'd probably be approached by someone at church or work and be asked about whether she'd seen this or that.

Hazel took a few deep breaths. *I have lots of time to see all kinds of things, and I will enjoy it all.*

She took out the brochure for the Palace of Holyrood, which she planned to tour after Parliament. Tours were available at the palace as long as the king was not in residence. Since Charles and Camilla were in Canada at the moment, Hazel anticipated a full tour.

On her way toward the main entry, she passed Parliament's modern lines of oak, steel, and granite. It was as if the architects of this structure had been determined not to allow their masterpiece to be fused into its ancient surroundings. This achievement was to stand out in its uniqueness and freshness, and to Hazel it certainly did.

Many people strolled about in the lobby, waiting for the tour to begin. Hazel immediately noticed a familiar face among them: the quiet man she had seen in the elevator. He had dressed casually again, as he had the previous evening, with jeans, hoodie, and that black backpack hanging down from his shoulder. Hazel thought of going over to say hello but then reconsidered; he hadn't seemed too friendly.

As she took the opportunity to study the glass-covered display cases in the lobby, a middle-aged man approached with a lanyard dangling in front of his tie.

"The tour will start in a few minutes," the man said, surveying the lobby. "We have a good crowd with us this mornin', so our tour should take aboot forty, maybe forty-five minutes. They call me Lance. I've been doin' this tour for years and have ne'er lost a visitor—yet."

A few chuckles bounced around the tourists.

Hazel expected the tour guide to begin by explaining the building's planning stages, perhaps as early as the 1980s. She felt disappointed when Lance began in the 1100s, a time when Scotland's King David I had built an abbey on this location; its nearby remains could be seen outside. The guide continued on to explain the area's history, which included the Palace of Holyrood, the official residence in Scotland for the British monarch. Hazel heard many familiar names such as Robert the Bruce, Mary Queen of Scots, John Knox, and Queen Victoria.

Lance extended his clipboard, like a pointer, toward the Parliament Café and the Parliament Shop as they proceeded through the lobby. They then ventured down a maze of hallways, pausing at various points of interest. Lance discussed controversies over the building's cost and modern design. Often he added interesting and humorous tidbits. Throughout, Hazel noticed smartly dressed government employees stopping to chat in a corridor, oblivious to the tour group.

Must be challenging to work in a place where tour groups pass all the time, she mused. *I suppose they've learned to ignore us.*

Most of the group kept pace with the guide, but Hazel perpetually found herself at the back, often arriving too late to catch all of Lance's remarks. She failed to catch many of his punchlines, only hearing the chuckles that followed. This had nothing to do with her sore knee, for by now she was walking quite well. But the detailed information conveyed via photos, maps, and drawings held her back. She wasn't dawdling; she was only trying to understand the history, read the complete story, and take a few photos. She refused to be rushed.

For Pete's sake, why is everyone in such a hurry? So annoying.

The group continued their way to the garden lobby, progressing down still more hallways and around other corners.

An elderly man with a cane often hung back as well, but never for long. He always hurried to catch up, moving surprisingly fast. He reminded Hazel of ninety-year-old Margaret at church.

The man from the hotel tended to lag as well. He too would pause to read the signage. If anything, he was even slower than she was.

Lance then explained that they were about to see the main level of the debating chamber. Hazel managed to hear him say that although today was a regular business day in the Scottish Parliament, no debate would be occurring in the impressive auditorium. Otherwise they could have witnessed Parliament in action.

Sunlight flooded the empty chamber. Like in a courtroom, the front held raised benches for the Speaker and parliamentary leaders to comfortably sit and address the members. They would look out upon the wooden desks and black swivel chairs, stretching in semi-circular rows that followed the curve of the auditorium.

Hazel glanced up at the vaulted glass ceiling supported by beautiful wooden beams. Lights and cameras hung from a network of metal rods and brackets.

They left the debating chamber and followed Lance up a flight of stairs, with a few people opting to take the elevator. Once out on the chamber's large balcony, all eyes surveyed the curved rows of attached wooden seats. To Hazel, they looked terribly uncomfortable.

The group was following their guide when Hazel heard voices below. Looking down, she noticed a woman and two men, probably government employees, chatting on the main level.

The tour continued along corridors without stopping, passing paintings by local artists. Hazel wished they could take a break to catch their collective breath. She paused at large photos showing the building's complex construction phases. Some showed a conglomeration of curved roofs of silver.

She suddenly turned and found herself alone. It was a repeat of the ordeal at Greyfriars the evening before. She tried to catch up with the group, but realized that she couldn't find them, not even the man with the cane or the slow-walking man from the hotel. She stood still, trying to detect the chatter of tourists or the distinct clip of shoes on granite flooring.

She heard nothing. She had gotten lost.

Hazel decided to take a minute or two to look further. If unsuccessful, she'd head back downstairs and enjoy the café and giftshop. After that, she would head over to explore the Palace of Holyrood.

She continued towards a point where the hall forked, choosing to go left. Hazel now believed the group was entirely out of reach. Having not the tiniest inkling which direction to take, she kept moving forward even though she felt uncomfortable. The design of this part of the building seemed very utilitarian, as though it hadn't been intended to be part of any tour. At least the hall seemed empty.

Hazel was about to turn around to head back the way she'd come when she caught a glimpse of movement up ahead. A shadow disappeared around the hallway's curve. She picked up her pace, feeling curious, but only encountered more and more empty hallways.

But then she heard a footstep and turned in time to catch sight of a backpack disappearing through a side door. Hazel felt instant relief. This must be the man from the hotel. He had been lagging behind, just like her. Maybe he too was trying to catch up with the others.

She followed him through the same doorway and realized that it led back out to the balcony overlooking the debating chamber.

*   *   *

Jean-Paul grew frustrated with the woman from his hotel and the old man with the cane, but he finally managed to remain far enough behind the tour group that he could depart and return to the balcony overlooking the debating chamber.

He tried to ignore thoughts of this being his last assignment. He wouldn't really feel at peace until this was all over, with him sitting on a plane high above Scotland. Such thoughts only made him more edgy.

He shoved them aside. He had a job to do. Last night he had studied the layout of Parliament. After meeting with his contact, a government employee, he felt more confident about the details of the assignment.

Jean-Paul cared little for either his contact or his target. The less he knew, the better. But as any professional would do in his position, he demanded specifics about several things: the rifle, the silencer, the range, the position, the exit.

He made a right turn and dashed through a side door, bringing him onto the empty balcony. He made his way between the rows of attached wooden seats and crouched next to the designated partition. Sufficiently obscured, he bent down to retrieve the stowed rifle, loaded and complete with attached silencer.

But that's not what he found. He pulled out a loaded revolver and saw what he thought must be the silencer lying off to the side.

The plan had called for a rifle, a long-range weapon for a long-range target. The politician he'd been hired to kill was standing below, between two others.

He stood up in disbelief, still holding the loaded revolver. He glanced back at his target, seething in anger at this turn of events. He couldn't carry out the assignment—not without a rifle and appropriate silencer. All had been compromised.

• • •

Hazel stepped onto the balcony, once again hearing the conversation of the employees below. She suspected it must be the same three people as before. She then glanced across the balcony and caught some movement on the far end.

There he is! The man from the hotel was unmistakable. *He's probably just as frustrated as I am.*

Hazel began approaching him, getting closer and closer. Maybe he'd be more friendly if he knew they were in the same situation.

When she stood about four metres behind him, she opened her mouth. "Hi there—"

Startled, the man turned and Hazel's eyes flew open at the realization that he was holding a revolver. He stepped back, but he caught his foot on a metal plate used to bolt a nearby seat to the floor.

She tried to turn away, but not before she saw him fall to the floor of the balcony.

In that moment, Hazel heard the crack of a revolver firing. The explosive shot echoed through the auditorium, bouncing off the high ceilings like surround sound in a movie theatre.

Hazel fell backward, her arms flung out in desperation to break her fall. She felt sharp pain as the back of her head hit the edge of an aisle seat. A different type of pain, even more excruciating, suddenly swept across her upper body.

As she slumped to the floor, she whispered, "Jesus, help…"

Glancing down, she saw a pool of red spread across her white shirt. She slipped into unconsciousness.

TWENTY-FIVE

Edinburgh

HAZEL OPENED HER eyes to unfamiliar surroundings, feeling as though she had been on a long journey. But where had she been and where was she now?

Her head turned to follow the sound of rhythmic pumping and was confronted by mounted screens to her left, as well as steel poles, bags of fluid, and plastic tubes. She tried to shift her position, but any movement brought on pain. She closed her eyes and listened to a distant conversation. The voices soothed her. She wasn't alone.

She attempted to assemble her random thoughts and memories like pieces of a puzzle, struggling to arrive at a cohesive and logical explanation. It proved too much work and she dozed off again.

• • •

Hours later, she opened her eyes, sensing the presence of someone standing nearby.

"Hello, Hazel. I'm Dr. McCallister. I'm sure ye must be feelin' disoriented, but ye are at the Western General Hospital. And doin' well."

Hazel remained silent, not knowing what to say. All she could do was stare at the young female doctor and the other woman and man, equally as young, standing beside her bed. She searched their faces for understanding.

What do you mean I'm doing well? What happened?

As if reading her mind, Dr. McCallister continued, "Ye were shot and—"

"Shot!" The strength of her own voice amazed her.

"Yes, and ye are recoverin' well. Ye've had emergency surgery to extract a bullet lodged in ye muscle, just grazin' the right side of ye collar bone. The procedure went well. Absolutely no complications. From ye're fall, ye suffered a concussion. We'll be watchin' that. Ye're on an IV right now for fluids, but we hope to get ye eatin' tomorrow. Might even try tonight. We'll see. I'll check back with ye in the mornin'. Do ye have any questions?"

A thousand questions swirled about in Hazel's mind, but she couldn't formulate even one.

"We know this must be a shock. It's not what people expect to happen to them on vacation. But if ye had a choice, ye picked a good place to be shot—just below the clavicle. Easy enough to deal with, and recovery looks great. We'll have ye up and walkin'. The sooner the better. If all looks good, ye may even be discharged later tomorrow. Not sure yet. We'll see."

The doctor turned to leave, her auburn ponytail swinging across her back. Her young man colleague followed behind but paused long enough to give Hazel a warm reassuring smile.

The third person, a nurse, remained at Hazel's bedside. She introduced herself as Ava as she busied herself studying Hazel's chart and checking the monitors.

Hazel couldn't believe she had been shot. Who would shoot her? She tried to piece together her last memories but found that her recollection contained gaps.

She finally voiced a question. "Do you know what happened to me?"

"From what I've heard, ye're in a group tourin' the Parliament buildin' this mornin'."

"Okay... I do remember that. Yes, I was lost, looking for the group, wasn't I? That man... from the same hotel as me... I followed him. He held a gun. He shot me?"

"I don't know any details. The main thing is that ye're recoverin' well. I've heard that the police may be by later today, maybe early evenin', to ask a few questions. Nothin' to worry about."

"The police?"

"Sorry, I don't know the details."

"You know, I can picture that man toppling onto those chairs, probably as I was falling. Must have really hurt himself. Do you think he'd be here?"

"I don't know. This afternoon, I think we'll see about gettin' ye standin' and walkin' around a wee bit."

The thought of walking made Hazel feel exhausted. What kind of nightmare had she fallen into?

While Ava checked her blood pressure and dressing, Hazel put aside her bewilderment and prayed for the man who had shot her.

Help him, God, to be okay. And help him with his life. He must be a criminal... then again, he could be an undercover cop. I have no idea.

"All looks good," Ava said. "How's ye pain control? I can increase ye morphine if you'd like?"

Hazel thought her pain was manageable as long as she stayed in bed.

As Ava turned to leave, she looked back at Hazel. "Ye must be lookin' forward to yer sister comin'? I love that name... *Fran*. Same name as my favourite aunt."

Hazel's eyes widened in shock.

"Oh, I'm sorry. I guess ye didn't know. Yes, yer sister is on her way over. Administration found yer passport information and called yer emergency contact. Always good to keep that kind of information handy."

Hazel sighed. "I think I will have a bit more morphine."

Before Ava left the room, she checked Hazel's temperature. "Ye're lookin' a little pale right now. I'm going to double-check a few things."

Only once she was satisfied that Hazel was stable did she finally leave, but not before Hazel asked about her purse and retrieved her phone.

Without considering the time change, Hazel immediately called her sister's landline. The phone rang several times before Roger hurriedly picked up.

"Hello," he said.

"Hi, Roger. It's me. Hazel."

"Hazel? Wow—Hazel! Good to hear your voice. If you're phoning, you must be doing okay, eh? In hospital and not a morgue." He paused, perhaps waiting for a laugh that never came. "So what on earth happened? I have a thousand questions."

Hazel offered a brief description of what she knew—that she'd been shot while out on a tour, but she could hardly relay much detail since she was still processing it herself.

"Is Fran really on her way over?" she blurted out. "Why?"

"I just got back from dropping her off. She got one of those red-eye flights. One-way to Edinburgh, believe it or not. She should arrive tomorrow afternoon your time. I'll text you her flight info if you'd like. Oh, I should let you know that she's already talked to your doctor—McCallister, is it?"

She nodded, forgetting momentarily that he couldn't see her.

"And then she called your travel insurance company," Roger continued. "That's being processed, as far as I know. Let's see... she also left a message at your church office, so they'll all be praying for you. She was going to leave a message at your work too but thought that could wait. Hopefully you'll recover well and be home soon."

More than physical pain, Hazel felt anger—and it was building. What did Fran think she was doing? She had no business interfering. Informing the entire world about what had happened? She had no business at all.

"You know, Hazel, Fran really does care about you a lot. I know you two are often like oil and water, but she worries about you. They called here when you were out of surgery and said they'd removed a bullet and that recovery looked good. Anyway, Fran flew into action mode—you know what she's like. She never did have a good feeling about you travelling alone in the first place. She's been worried about you travelling ever since she first heard of your plans."

"She always seemed more annoyed with me than worried."

"Well, she does worry. And hearing about what happened, well… it got her into a real frenzy. She rearranged her commitments this week, and before we knew it she had me drive her to the airport."

Hazel no longer knew what to feel or think, but Roger had more questions. Hazel shared everything she could, then reassured him that she would be fine, that the medical staff was doing everything they could. In fact, she might be discharged as early as the next day.

"Well, that will be good," Roger said. "And Fran will be there to help you."

Hazel ignored this and ended the call by at least thanking Roger for his concern.

Afterward she lay in bed, realizing she had never heard Roger talk so much. She pictured Fran getting huffy and puffy while rearranging her entire week. Thoughts of her sister flapping around almost produced a smile.

But she dreaded the next few days with Fran at her side, especially since her help wasn't needed.

When Ava returned, she arranged several pillows around Hazel's neck and back, allowing her to sit up more comfortably. Between the fall on cobblestone and the fall at Parliament, Hazel was glad to feel the morphine slowly kick in.

With the remaining charge on her cellphone, Hazel brought up a game of solitaire. At times she would hit *undo* when a bad move destined her to lose.

How marvellous it would be if I could undo moves in my own life. Like maybe I could have taken a castle tour instead of Parliament. My life right now would be so different. But I can't. I can't undo anything. Lord, help me deal with this—this recovery, this vacation, this visit from Fran… What a mess.

She went back over all the preparations she'd taken in advance of the trip. She recalled visiting that store in Calgary, looking for items related to travel. They should have sold bulletproof vests.

Ava's shift ended early in the evening and Trish came on duty.

"Hi, I'm Trish," the new nurse said. "I'll be lookin' after ye tonight. Umm, also the police are in the hallway and are here to ask ye a few questions."

Two police officers entered a few moments later. The older male officer and his younger female partner had pleasant smiles and seemed genuinely concerned for Hazel's well-being.

Hazel had rehearsed what she could remember, not wanting to come across as a useless, incompetent witness. She refused to be like the many characters she tolerated on her regular crime shows. She searched her mind for vital information.

None of the details she supplied seemed to surprise or interest them very much. It turned out they already knew most of it and had already determined this was likely a case of a tourist being caught in the wrong place at the wrong time.

But right at the end of the interview, one piece of information did get their attention.

"That man was staying at the same hotel as I was," Hazel remembered. "I saw him a couple of times yesterday. I also think he has a French accent." She paused, biting her lip. "But I didn't mean to startle him. Do you know if he's okay?"

The officers didn't give Hazel an answer but added their wishes for a good recovery and left the room. Not long after, she slept fitfully for seven hours, waking up each time a nurse came in to check on her.

• • •

Jean-Paul lay handcuffed to his bed in the emergency room. Not long after the prompt arrival of police and ambulance to the scene of the shooting, he had been arrested and taken here for treatment, where he remained uncommunicative.

He hardly needed the handcuffs, for he had sustained several incapacitating injuries, from a concussion and sprained arm to cracked ribs and a sprained ankle. He hoped the police didn't figure out who he really was. At least for the time being, his identity remained a mystery. He carried a Spanish passport and various false details. As for his backpack, it contained only a few essentials like clothing and toiletries. And as for the burner phone? It had already been wiped clean.

TWENTY-SIX

Edinburgh

IT HAD BEEN twenty-four hours since the shooting and Hazel was recovering well, her diet having transitioned from liquids to solids and her movements graduating to a walking shuffle. Several times she made her way along the hospital corridor, aiming for the lounge at the end. She complied with the request of every nurse, determined to recover quickly and be dependent on Fran for nothing. She would do jumping jacks if they asked her to.

By late afternoon, a conversation outside Hazel's door woke her from a nap. She hoped it was the doctor and nurse discussing her discharge plans, but the conversation soon escalated to a disagreement, the loud exchange even bordering on a scuffle.

As Hazel opened her eyes, Fran appeared in the doorway, her suitcase dragged behind her on its rattling wheels. Close on her heels came a man carrying a bouquet of pink miniature roses.

"Fran…" She suddenly recognized the man. "George?"

"Hi ye lassie." George stepped around Fran, shooting her a satisfied glance as though to say, *See, she does know me.* "Terrible news to hear ye'd been shot. What a thing to happen to ye. I wanted to come by and give ye these. Brighten things up for ye."

"Thank you, George. These are beautiful! So kind of you." She smiled at her admirer. "I'm doing okay, and I'm on the mend. Should be out of the hospital soon, probably tomorrow. Depends on what the doctor says. They don't keep people in very long nowadays, do they?" She made quick eye contact with her sister, who seemed annoyed. "Oh, George, this is my sister Fran. She just arrived from Canada."

Stony looks and stilted nods were exchanged.

"I won't keep ye. Best be on my way, but ye get well now." With a smile and an affectionate nod, George left.

Speechless, Fran watched George go before turning her full attention to her sister. She talked while dragging a chair over toward Hazel's bedside.

"Well, when I thought you would have a challenging vacation, I wasn't thinking it would be like this—getting shot! And then some stranger bringing you flowers. What on earth happened?"

Not waiting for an answer, Fran bent over to give Hazel an awkward but gentle hug. She sat and waited expectantly to be informed.

Hazel summarized her tour of the Scottish Parliament, followed by a medical update. "The nurses say I'm doing well. Whenever they discharge me, I'm to come back in a few days to have the wound checked." She let out a long sigh. "You know, Fran, you really didn't need to come."

"Well, I can tell you that a trip to Scotland certainly wasn't on my agenda. But somehow the importance of preparing for the summer book sale faded when the hospital phoned me."

"But I'm sure they told you that I was okay?"

"Dear Hazel, *shot* and *okay* don't go well together... but you're right, I knew you weren't at death's door. At that point they didn't know how long you'd be in hospital, how quickly the wound would heal, and then a concussion, etcetera, etcetera. I wondered how you would manage getting around, especially getting home. It was clear to me that you needed help. And here I am."

Hazel knew Fran would have been forced to rearrange endless details to be here. "How many things did you have to rearrange?"

"That doesn't matter… a lot actually. But everything is covered. And I'm here now to help get you home."

The thought of going home hadn't crossed Hazel's mind—only how to carry on with her vacation. She'd intended to go home on her return flight as scheduled, not until July 18.

"Once I'm discharged, I should be fine to carry on with my vacation. Much slower, of course."

"We'll see how things go."

What does that mean? she wondered to herself. *This is my vacation, Fran. My life. I'm staying for my entire vacation, no matter what. You can't possibly be thinking of staying that long?*

Hazel made a quick calculation. Four vacation days had already swept by—two for travel, one to flounder in the rain, and another to get shot. That left ten remaining days. If Fran intended to stay that long, the whole trip would be ruined.

Maybe after a day or two, she'll see how well I'm doing and fly back to her busy life.

"You may as well stay in my hotel," Hazel suggested.

"That's what they said when I called them. I've arranged to have the room next to yours once you're discharged. They were extremely accommodating."

Hazel sighed again as she looked past Fran to a hospital worker carrying her dinner tray into the room. Hazel ate her chicken and pasta while Fran fished out a granola bar from her bag.

After dinner, Hazel felt tired, but Fran soon drifted off, leaning awkwardly in the bedside chair.

Hazel looked at her sister and considered how vulnerable she seemed while asleep. How limited the human body was. She smiled, thinking of the effort Fran had spent getting to Edinburgh.

I guess, deep down, she really does care for me.

● ● ●

Midmorning the next day, at the hospital, the sisters walked down the hallway to the lounge and eventually took the elevator to a café on the main floor. They both ordered lattes. While waiting for their drinks, awkwardness hung in the air. How odd it felt to be sitting next to Fran in a hospital café across the Atlantic. How strange life could be at times!

Fran broke the silence. "You know, Hazel, I remember saying something to you about going on such a vacation. *Reckless* was the word I think I used."

"Yes, it was. I remember your words quite clearly."

"Well, what I didn't say is that, besides reckless, I also thought it rather adventurous—in a reckless kind of way, of course."

"So what are you saying? You think I'm adventurous?"

Fran smiled for the first time since her arrival. "I suppose I am. You know, I was really scared there for a moment, scared that I'd lose you. Even though they assured me you were okay. I mean, you could take a turn for the worse. And where would I be? Thousands of miles away. So I wanted to get here as soon as I could."

Were those tears beginning to form in her sister's eyes?

"I appreciate your concern, Fran. I really do."

The rest of the conversation grew light, dwelling on the Scottish culture all around them.

On their way back to Hazel's room, Fran made a sudden stop in front of the hospital giftshop. "You don't mind if we stop here for a second?"

"Not at all."

Fran sorted through several sizes of boxed shortbread cookies. After assessing all options, she purchased three large boxes.

"So have you done any shopping yet?" Fran asked on their way back to the room.

"I bought a lovely scarf. I'll have to show you. And a Robert Burns poetry book."

"Well, good for you! I've only been in this country for a day and I've seen all kinds of things I'd love to get."

Later that afternoon, on another walk, Hazel talked about George. "He works at the hotel in maintenance. He's quite sweet, isn't he?"

"Well, I don't know about that," Fran retorted. "You just met him. And here he is, bringing you flowers. Anyway, you're fifty-five, so I'm not about to give you advice."

Hazel smiled. "Okay, sounds good." Maybe she imagined it, but she thought she detected another smile—a faint one—on Fran's face.

Once Hazel was back in bed, the discussion focused on their plans for the next few days. Fran had made it clear that she wouldn't be going home without Hazel, so she had booked a return flight for July 18.

Hazel didn't know how to respond other than to ask for God's ongoing help.

"You know, Hazel, part of me admires you. I mean, I've already mentioned you becoming adventurous. And when I look at you, well... not with your bruises and bandages, but really look at you... you booked a vacation and flew over here, on your own, completely out of your depth. No routine, and I know how much you love routine. You're exploring a new culture, walking around castles, cathedrals, and ancient museums. It takes courage to do something like that on your own. I know this past year hasn't been easy for you, with Julie's death, but I admire you for carrying on with your life. I'm proud of you, even though this silly business of travelling alone wasn't the best idea."

Hazel appreciated Fran's words of encouragement and dismissed the rest. "Several things helped me consider travelling. Of course Julie's death crushed me. We were such good friends. Did everything together. But I let my life shrink. And then my neighbour Praveen died this spring. He was such a nice man. Back in the fall, of course, there was Aunt Peggy's funeral. She did a lot, didn't she? And I hardly knew her. In comparison, my life seemed shallow. And when I was driving home from her funeral, I was almost hit by a truck."

"Hit by a truck?"

"Yes. A turquoise one. It sailed through a red light, missing me by millimetres. That really shook me up. I began to think how death can come at any moment. I could be gone just like that! And what would I have lived for? My funeral oration would be short: 'She basically did nothing with her life but made it a comfortable one.'"

"Well, that's not true," Fran shot back. "You're helping all the time. You help at your church. You help your company. I mean, where would those people be without your hard work? You're so good with numbers and finances."

"If I had a nickel every time someone told me that, I'd have a million dollars and eighty-five cents."

They chuckled together, and Hazel felt the proverbial ice melting. She couldn't remember a time when they had shared with each other to this extent. She felt happy and hopeful. She'd prayed about her relationship with Fran but had never pictured them laughing together—certainly not in Scotland, of all places.

The discussion stopped abruptly with the arrival of Dr. McAllister, who brought the welcome news that Hazel would be discharged as soon as the paperwork was completed. She advised Hazel to return to hospital in the next few days to check the wound.

The paperwork took a while. Upon receiving it, Fran asked multiple questions that took them into the early evening. As difficult as these days were going to be, Hazel at least knew she would be well looked after, with Fran ensuring every iota of instructions were followed.

By the time the sisters left the hospital, it was almost seven o'clock in the evening. Fran helped Hazel into a taxi.

They entered the lobby of the hotel. George, having apparently worked overtime, appeared as if on cue. The three of them chatted and Hazel couldn't help but notice Fran and George interacting more warmly.

The sisters took the elevator to their rooms, where Fran helped Hazel get settled.

"Now, are you feeling, okay?" Fran asked as Hazel got into bed. "Do you need any painkillers?"

Hazel didn't let this bother her. She knew her sister Fran had nothing else to do but look after her. Aside from texting updates to Roger and Ben, not to mention members of her church community, she had nothing to arrange—nothing to do at all. Hazel was the one and only item on her agenda.

. . .

The next day, because Hazel felt well-rested and was anxious to get back to exploring, Fran ordered a taxi to Edinburgh Castle. The sisters, Hazel in a beige top and Fran in a blouse of multi-coloured geometric shapes, looked out the taxi windows as they drew closer to the castle, perched high atop the rocky hill that dominated the city.

At the entry, waiting in a lineup to pay, Fran read from Hazel's brochure about the many famous people who were associated with the castle's history: Margaret Tudor, Mary Queen of Scots, James VI, Oliver Cromwell, and Sir Walter Scott.

When they neared the cashier, they both turned toward the grand stone archway at the sound of droning bagpipes. Everyone in the line turned to watch and listen to the young piper in full regalia.

Hazel was ecstatic. "Isn't this magnificent? It's the sound of Scotland!"

"It's certainly loud," Fran replied over the drone of the pipes. "Not my kind of thing, but you're right, it's so Scottish. But we're English through and through…"

The sisters spent the morning walking around the castle, taking the steep stone inclines slowly. They toured the parts of the castle built for royalty: the Crown Room and Royal Palace, the Great Hall, and St. Margaret's Chapel. They took the stairs down to the darkened places built for prisoners, although neither sister wanted to linger there. Hazel was fine not to read too much detail about what life had been like down here.

They sat down for lunch at the castle's Redcoat Café. Not before Hazel could order herself a coffee, Fran waved her arm to catch a waiter's attention.

"Yes, we'd like a large pot of tea. Earl Grey would be lovely." Smiling, she turned to Hazel. "What a fascinating place! That Great Hall is so splendid—the javelins, suits of armour... and what a fireplace! I love the rich, rusty colour of the wall. I think it would look perfect in my office."

Hazel had been longing for a coffee after all their exploring and felt irritated at Fran for taking over the order and getting tea for two. With every sip of tea, her tastebuds would protest. But she chose to let it go at the sight of her sister's beaming face. She seemed so happy.

During lunch, Hazel took a chance to ask Fran a question that had been on her mind for a while.

"Fran, do you know why I'm really here?"

"What do you mean? You're here on vacation."

"There's a bit more to it."

Fran looked both curious and bemused. "Let me guess. You're a government spy on assignment and got shot in the line of duty?"

Hazel smiled and began her story. She told about Mr. Lee insisting that she take vacation time. Then she backed up to September, when she'd found herself feeling down about life. She explained about the original receipt, then detailed each subsequent one, ending with Praveen's.

Fran listened, often smiling. She laughed about the caramel macchiato and sports bag.

At one point Fran laughed so hard that she almost choked on her soup. Encouraged, Hazel shared a few more details, hoping to hear that laugh again. She went on to reveal the disappointment she'd felt upon failing to get to Jedburgh. She also spoke of the text from Maddie about the possibility of Evergreen going out of business, not to mention Hazel's fall on the cobblestones. The story concluded with the rain driving her into St. Giles' Cathedral, where she'd surrendered her future, her job, her everything to God.

"I feel so silly about the receipts," she confessed at the very end.

"Hazie, you don't need to feel silly. You used the receipts to get out and do things. Nothing wrong with that. It's not *so* crazy, when you think about it. You were just responding to a form of advertising. You read about something and then made a choice about what to do with that info. You got yourself out of a rut… and now here you are in Europe."

"Thanks, Fran."

As they made their way back to the hotel, they discussed their plans for the following morning. They wanted to tour the Palace of Holyrood, which would probably consume their entire day.

Once settled in bed again, Hazel wrote in her prayer journal with a thankful heart to God. Her comments today mostly went under the "Fran" column.

Before going to sleep, though, she heard a knock on her door. She got up and looked through the peephole. On the other side, Fran was staring back with a serious expression, still wearing her gaudy blouse.

The moment she opened the door, Fran began talking.

"Hazie, I've been thinking, and I've done some research. I have a different plan for tomorrow."

TWENTY-SEVEN

Paris

ON BASTILLE DAY, Brielle arrived at Marie's apartment early. She stood in the entryway, wearing a royal blue silk jacket over off-white pants and a top. The minute Brielle entered, she felt nervous and fidgeted with her cellphone.

"I haven't heard from him, Marie," Brielle began. She found herself speaking in short sentences. "He should have been back by now. Tuesday, he said. But I've called and called. No answer. Nothing. What's happened? I'm so worried."

Marie looked worried and Brielle couldn't blame her; she must seem so distraught and pale.

"Something obviously came up, Brielle," Marie assured her. "He'll probably show up in the next hour or so. Late, but that's okay. Here, you need orange juice or coffee. You need… well, I don't know what you need. Come sit down."

Marie led her over to a corner sofa chair.

Brielle's hands shook, and Marie soon brought her a cup of coffee, setting it on the side table alongside a plain croissant. It wasn't quite the same as her favourite pain au chocolat. But when

Brielle considered her shaking hands, her white outfit, and the chocolate, she thought that maybe it was for the best.

Hopefully this would all pass once Jean-Paul arrived.

"I don't understand it." Brielle rested a hand on her pocket, feeling her phone and the lifeline to her son it represented. "He promised he'd be here—*pas un problème*, right? It's not as if he's that far away. He didn't go to Los Angeles or New York. Just Scotland. So what's happened?"

Brielle took out her phone and dialled her son's number again, to no avail.

Despite Marie's efforts, they didn't say another word. Marie just busied herself with the task of ensuring all the food and drinks would be ready for the guests to arrive—and that would happen within the hour.

Guests soon filled the apartment with laughter, conversation, and life. Several people filled their plates with breakfast items and took them out to the balcony where the sky beamed blue. Not a cloud in sight.

Brielle greeted a few friends, but then slipped away to Marie's den where she could close the door and quietly try phoning Jean-Paul again.

After several failed calls, she made a choice. She stood up and, cloaking herself with stoic dignity, moved to join the party.

Suddenly, her phone chimed.

"Hello?" she answered breathlessly.

It wasn't Jean-Paul on the other end of the line, but someone representing him. Brielle didn't quite understand what the strange man was saying.

And when she finally did grasp the message, she almost fainted. She opened the door and staggered into the frame, her face ashen.

Marie rushed over and led her to a chair. Someone brought a glass of water. Another person called for Claude, who had been a family doctor back in the day. Before long, she was also handed a damp cloth and glass of port.

"It's Jean-Paul…" Brielle's whisper was so quiet, no one could hear.

Marie prompted her to speak louder.

"Edinburgh. *C'est incroyable.* Terrible." She drew a deep, shuddering breath. "He's been… arrested…"

Her hand rose to her forehead as if to ward off a migraine.

"And he's in hospital. Broken arm, ribs. Arrested. How can… how can that be?"

Brielle broke down into heavy sobs.

TWENTY-EIGHT

Edinburgh

EVEN BEFORE FRAN could share her plan, Hazel rebelled. "No Fran, we already made plans. This is *my* vacation and I want to see the Palace of Holyrood."

But Fran pushed open the door and swept into the room. "Hazel, I've done some research. I've put myself in your shoes and asked myself, 'Now, what would I do? What would I want?'"

"What do you mean?"

Fran sat down on the edge of the bed. Hazel grudgingly sat beside her.

"We should go to Jedburgh! I know there's a train strike on, which really messes things up. I looked at the bus routes and all the connections, but a person recovering from being shot doesn't need that! So I suggest we go to Jedburgh by taxi. It can take us right to your store. And Hazel, I want to pay for this. I don't want a penny from you—it's my treat. Afterwards there's some old abbey to see, and a house where Mary Queen of Scots lived—she sure gets around, doesn't she? Coming back, we could have dinner in little old Tweedbank—such a cute name. Anyway, I'm game if you are."

"Fran, I'm not…" Hazel paused, looking up at the ceiling, "How do I say this? I don't care about the receipt. Not anymore. I don't care about umbrellas. I'm free from all that now. I appreciate your research, but I don't need to go to Jedburgh."

"I know. I know. And that's why I think you *should* go—because you no longer *need* to. Look, Hazie, we are different from each other in so many ways, but in some ways we are so much alike. We both like things neat and tidy, we like to get things done, we like to keep organized and cross things off our lists. I mean, why not go? It would complete your receipt adventure. You'll have finished something no other human being has ever done—follow through with five receipts. And besides, you'll get to the exact place where Praveen went. I know you don't *need* to go, but perhaps you *want* to go."

Hazel fell silent, thinking about the idea. It felt good to want something instead of needing it. She especially thought about Praveen and the joy of following in his footsteps.

"It will give you a sense of completion," Fran continued. "It's an accomplishment. Otherwise it might fester like an agenda item never dealt with. And it's totally doable. What do you think? We still have lots of time to explore the rest of Edinburgh and Hollywood or whatever it's called. So let's go see some Scottish countryside. We'll have fun."

The more Hazel thought about her sister's plan, the more favourable it seemed. It *would* complete her adventure quite nicely.

And I know I don't need to. But I think I want to.

"I don't need another umbrella," Hazel pointed out. "I just bought one and I already have one at home. How many does a person need?"

"At least three."

. . .

Early the next morning, the sisters stood outside their hotel in the bright sun. Their taxi pulled up after a few minutes, ready to take them on a two-hour trip to Jedburgh.

When not looking out at the rolling green valleys dotted with ruins, the sisters talked. And talked. And talked.

"I'm trying not to worry about my job," Hazel remarked as a particularly scenic set of castle ruins flew by. "If the business does close, I have to believe God has a plan for me."

"Of course he does. Maybe you could work in a bank. Or start your own accounting company, doing income tax—that would suit you. Or you could try something completely different. And if the situation gets desperate, remember that Roger and I have a huge basement. Whatever happens, I won't allow you to become homeless. Don't worry, God will provide."

Their conversation spanned their decades together. They reminisced about their previous summertime travels with their parents. They each recalled different highlights the other had forgotten.

"And here we are travelling about, touring Scotland," Hazel remarked. "I'm not glad that I got shot, but I'm glad you're here."

"Me too, Hazel."

"You know, we haven't always been very close as sisters. I'm glad we can do this together."

"I guess we've both been busy with our lives. Me especially, always overcommitting myself. Perhaps it's time we change things. Try getting together more than just for Christmas. Like for Thanksgiving at your place. That was really nice."

"I agree. We need to do more things like that."

Fran turned to study her more closely. "What is it with this George guy? You're not going to start a long-distance relationship, are you?"

"Fran, we're just friends! Of course, we do have each other's email by now... so we can, you know, stay in touch. As friends. Oh, and I forgot to mention that he'd like to drive us to the airport next week." Hazel found herself babbling on as if she couldn't help it. "You must admit that he's a lovely man, isn't he? He's so polite and interesting. He looks like the detective in that British series—can't remember the name, but it's the detective who likes sailing. George looks like a sailor, doesn't he? Can't you just picture George in a grey turtleneck sailing the high seas?"

Fran shot a worried look at her sister, adrift in thought. Lost at sea.

• • •

After their scenic drive, they reached the town late in the morning and stood outside a giftshop. A curved wooden banner above the door read *Jedburgh Royal Gifts*. After capturing the doorframe and banner on her camera, Hazel stood back from it, amazed that she had finally arrived.

"Well, I don't know what you're waiting for!" Fran said as she entered the store, with Hazel following.

Fran wasted no time and began doing serious shopping with a basket in hand.

Hazel didn't immediately start searching for umbrellas. She was too busy luxuriating in the feeling of accomplishment.

Fran was right. I'm here. I can't believe I made it!

She walked around in silent prayer, glad to have arrived at this place where she wanted to visit but no longer needed to. And yet God had brought her here anyway—and with Fran, of all people.

Hazel thought about Praveen and wondered what had brought him to this town—this out-of-the-way place. What had made him buy an umbrella here? Where had he come from and where had he been going? She knew she would never know the answers and had to be content with the unknown.

Before heading to the umbrella display, Hazel noticed Fran snapping up hoodies.

They're probably for Roger, Ben, and Megan, she thought, shaking her head. *She's going to need to buy another suitcase.*

Hazel approached a table that held rows of compact umbrellas, each one in its nylon-clasped covering. She picked up several, checking inside since the outside covering didn't always match the interior. She quickly dismissed anything loud and bright.

One umbrella did catch her eye. Once out of its covering, Hazel opened it fully to admire the pattern. She didn't know if Fran was in hearing distance, but in her excitement it didn't matter.

"Fran, look!" she exclaimed rather loudly.

Fran, who stood at a nearby display of soaps and hand creams, came alongside.

"Look at it, Fran." Hazel's voice had gone back to normal. "I love the black and grey and little red lines. So classy. It's lovely… and it's tartan."

"It's absolutely perfect, Hazie."

TWENTY-NINE

Paris

BRIELLE WALKED INTO the Latin Quarter, along the winding cobblestones of Rue de la Huchette. She had always loved this ancient street that had emerged during the Roman Empire. She especially enjoyed it now in late August as the tourist season ebbed.

She spotted Marie just ahead, shaking her head at a tacky display of souvenirs. The friends then turned to enter a nearby restaurant. Since Bastille Day, their luncheons had become more frequent.

In the early days after Jean-Paul's arrest, Brielle had felt trapped in a whirlwind of emotions. Marie would sit and listen to her friend's confusion, anger, and even guilt—every negative emotion a mother could feel. They shared many questions, but few answers. What had made Jean-Paul turn to a life of crime? Had it been the lure of money?

Over the course of the summer, Brielle had tried to see Jean-Paul, seeking to understand his tragic downfall. But he refused to see her. His only communication with his mother had come through his lawyer, whose frequent updates at least kept her informed on Jean-Paul's well-being. He seemed to be "doing all right," whatever that meant.

"Is there any chance this has all been a mistake?" Brielle had asked the lawyer. "Perhaps they got the wrong man?"

"No, Madame Desjardins. He's confessed to the attempted murder of an employee of the Scottish government. He is guilty and says so. Investigators believe he's involved in organized crime. The truth is that we're talking about murder—many murders. You must understand: Jean-Paul will be in prison for the rest of his life."

As Brielle and Marie sat in the restaurant, they fell into a comfortable silence. They had grown weary of rehashing the possibilities of what had gone so catastrophically wrong in Jean-Paul's life.

"He still refuses to see me, Marie," Brielle said at last.

Marie took a sip of her coffee. "He'll see you when he's ready, Brielle. But at least they've brought him back to Paris. When he does want to see you, it should be straightforward. You won't have to visit some prison outside of France, n'est-ce pas?"

After their lunch in the Latin Quarter, the friends parted ways. That's when Brielle received a call from the prison chaplain. She made her way to a nearby park bench to take the call.

Following a lengthy conversation, she crossed the bridge onto Île de la Cité and stopped in front of Notre Dame. It stood magnificently, just as it had always done since its completion in 1345. As if the fire of 2019 had never happened. Its repairs now complete, she watched as tourists and locals alike flocked to its doors.

Brielle decided it was time for her to do likewise.

Once inside, she stood amazed by the cathedral's brightness. But then, she had known it would be bright. She'd kept up with the news over the past years and how cleaning the stone walls and stained-glass windows had removed centuries of accumulated dirt and candle smoke.

She walked toward the front altar and took a seat to reflect upon the chaplain's words.

"Madame Desjardins, your son will see you soon, maybe next week," he had told her. "He and I have talked many times over the past month and had good spiritual conversations about his life and what it can become. I believe he can live the balance of his life with purpose. There is light in all of this... and it only takes a small amount of light to dispel darkness. Not everything is dark, Madame Desjardins."

Brielle looked over at one of the cathedral's three rose windows, their beauty magnified by sunlight. She thanked God, for she knew his hand had been at work. God had answered her prayers, although in the most painful way. Because of the choices he had made, Jean-Paul would spend the rest of his life in prison. But he still had a life to live, and she would be there to encourage him. There would be many dark and difficult days ahead, for them both, but she agreed with the chaplain that there was light in all of this.

"Il y a de la lumière," she whispered.

She left Notre Dame and strolled aimlessly along the Seine, thinking about her life. Even having just turned seventy-eight, she believed that a person could reinvent their life. She needed a new direction. Knowing she could no longer do much for Jean-Paul, other than visit him when he was ready, she longed to be involved in something worthwhile—to do something good and purposeful.

Her practice of stepping into churches throughout the city had opened Brielle's eyes to active ministries throughout Paris, from projects in art restoration to reaching out to the poor. The church where Marie's granddaughter had gotten married now operated an impressive outreach to the needy by means of a soup kitchen. Currently, they needed volunteers on certain mornings to prepare meals and she'd already decided to investigate the possibilities.

She couldn't help but smile at the thought of dragging Marie along. She imagined them working together, confident that Marie would eventually agree to this. As long as they went out for lunch afterwards.

THIRTY

Calgary

ON WEDNESDAY, THE last day of August, Hazel sat at her desk with three minutes left until closing. She flipped the page of her wall calendar, upending August's sandy path leading toward the ocean and secured September's cobblestone path toward an ancient stone building. So very Scottish.

She remained at her desk for several minutes, thinking about her job—a job that in four months' time would no longer exist. On her first day back from vacation, Mr. Lee had invited her to take a seat in his office. For the next twenty minutes, he'd explained his choice to retire and close down the business.

"But not till the end of December, which gives everyone ample time to look for other employment," he'd said. "I'll need you not only to handle the upcoming year-end, but also the accounting details of shutting down for good. Having never done this before, I'm not sure what it entails. But we'll work through it together."

Hazel had taken the news well, having expected it.

What she hadn't expected was being invited by Maddie into the coffee room right afterward. Hazel had followed her, worried that something might be wrong with the coffeemaker.

But instead she'd entered to find a freshly brewed pot of coffee on the table alongside a large two-layer cake slathered in vanilla icing, with the words "Welcome Back Hazel!" written in dark chocolate.

The coffee room had never been meant to hold the entire staff, but all nine people managed to stand inside its confines that morning, eating cake, drinking coffee, and chatting. Everyone had wanted to know the details of Hazel's vacation—especially the part about getting shot, of course.

Hazel tidied up her desk and left the office.

On the bus ride home, she considered taking a long walk after supper. She needed to get into shape for a hike around the Lower Kananaskis Lake that a group of four other women from church were planning.

I hope someone knows where to park and where the trailhead is, she thought. *I'm sure Julie will be looking down at us and laughing.*

Hazel exited the bus and walked to her apartment building. In the lobby, at her mailbox, she let out a satisfied sigh and tossed several glossy advertisements into the blue bin.

While heating up some chicken and rice leftovers that night, Hazel received a text from Fran that produced a smile, and almost a laugh.

"I need your prayers!!! Megan's mother and I are meeting for lunch next week. My idea. I must be mad!"

Hazel texted back. "Not mad Fran, but brave—very brave. Will be praying."

The sisters had fallen into a relaxed rhythm of texting since coming home from Scotland. Sometimes Hazel initiated. ("How did Ben and Megan like their hoodies?") Other times it was Fran. ("It's supposed to rain this afternoon—hope you use your new umbrella!")

Hazel knew Fran would always have an assertive edge. She'd always be busy leading and delegating. She was good at it and enjoyed that role. She'd always be Fran.

She realized that they could never change the past, but Hazel felt such joy in knowing that they had agreed to change their present relationship. Their middle-age years would be closer than their childhood years. They were building a strong sisterly bond—a relationship to treasure and maintain for the rest of their lives.

While Hazel ate, she thought through her plans for the rest of the evening. After a walk around the park, she would begin reviewing the church's financial statements. Although she wouldn't officially become the church bookkeeper until January 1, she wanted to be as prepared as possible. After all, this was a paid position.

Knowing she had a job in the new year had her marvelling at the way God answered her prayers. She felt privileged to look back over the last year and appreciate how God had orchestrated everything, bringing about answers to her prayers for adventure, purpose, and her relationship with Fran.

How astounding. It's simply astounding.

After supper, before going for her walk, she stepped out onto the balcony and felt the autumn breeze. The seasons were in transition and the days waffled back and forth between warm and cool. Already the temperature had dropped significantly since she'd gotten off the bus.

Hazel watched the tall grass across the street bend as the winds picked up. Looking north, she noticed heavy rainclouds on the horizon.

Well, maybe she'd get in a walk tomorrow.

She felt a twinge of disappointment. From her current view, she wasn't able to fully marvel in God's ability to create these weather elements, nor the fact that they always remained at his disposal—instruments to use as he so desired.

She turned her back on the wind and approaching rain and went inside.

That evening, as Hazel updated her prayer journal and thought more upon her year of answered prayer, she confessed to herself that there remained many things she couldn't see. Her limited vision didn't allow her to anticipate answers to her other prayers, many of which she had long forgotten she had even prayed. For example, her prayer for the murderer in Calgary to be caught, her prayer for the spiritual wellbeing of the person who had lost that first restaurant receipt, and her prayer for God to help the man who had shot her.

No, she didn't understand everything. But one day she hoped to better appreciate how God, in caring for her desires and hearing every word she spoke in faith, could change the trajectories of human lives to bring about his good and perfect will.

Now to him who is able to do immeasurably more than all we ask or imagine, according to his power that is at work within us, to him be glory in the church and in Christ Jesus throughout all generations, for ever and ever! Amen.
—Ephesians 3:20–21

ALSO WRITTEN BY
KIM LOUISE CLARKE

The French Collection: Moments with God in Paris

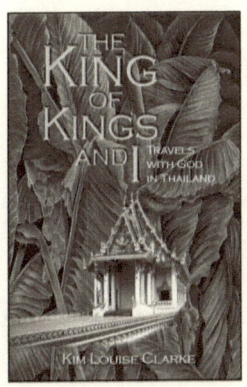

The King of Kings and I: Travels with God in Thailand

ABOUT THE AUTHOR

KIM LOUISE CLARKE'S goal in writing is to draw people to Jesus Christ through stories she hopes will inspire, inform, and entertain. *Prayers and Paper Trails* is her third book, which won the 2025 Braun Book Award for fiction with Word Alive Press. Her first two books, travel devotional memoirs based in Paris and Thailand, were shortlisted for the Women's Journey of Faith, also associated with Word Alive Press. Her other published works include articles, essays, devotionals, and contributions to anthologies.

Kim's writing is influenced and enriched by her Bachelor's degree in Religious Education from Prairie College. She has also been an active member of InScribe Christian Writers' Fellowship for fifteen years. She loves to travel, especially in Europe. She lives in Calgary, conveniently near the airport, with her husband of thirty-seven years. Kim has five adult children—a daughter, a son, and three stepsons.

www.ingramcontent.com/pod-product-compliance
Lightning Source LLC
Chambersburg PA
CBHW031228260626
47169CB00007B/2198